DRAGON'S FATE

THE DRAGON SHIFTER'S MATES #4

EVA CHASE

INK SPARK PRESS

Dragon's Fate

Book 4 in the Dragon Shifter's Mates series

This is a work of fiction. Any resemblance to actual persons, living or dead, or actual events is purely coincidental.

First Digital Edition, 2018

Cover design: Another World Designs

Ebook ISBN: 978-1-989096-01-7

Paperback ISBN: 978-1-989096-04-8

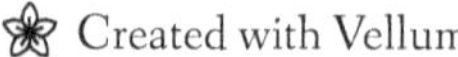 Created with Vellum

CHAPTER 1

Ren

As the private jet soared down toward the canine shifter estate, resolve sat tight and heavy in my chest. I should have been arriving here to meet the last group of shifter-kin as the newly confirmed mate of their alpha. I should have been bringing good news. I was their dragon shifter—the last dragon shifter alive. By taking the four alphas of the kin-groups as my mates, I was supposed to unite all shifter kind and end the turmoil they'd all been through.

Instead I'd have to announce that we might be on the verge of a paranormal war. That was what Marco, the feline alpha I'd consummated my mate-bond with less than a day ago, had called it. And I hadn't consummated my bond with the canine alpha yet. Sitting in the seats closest to the jet's door, West looked even more grim and tense than usual.

We'd been through plenty of turmoil already, but this time it was worse. Before, it'd just been our own kind we'd had to fight, rogue shifters who wanted to disrupt the status quo. Now, the remaining members of the rogues' sort-of pack had fled to the vampires, and the vampires, for whatever reason, had decided to attack us.

All we knew for sure was that the bloodsuckers had taken over a house that Marco's feline kin used as a local base of operations near New York City. He'd told his kin who'd survived the attack to meet us here, at the closest shifter estate nearby.

My hands clenched as the plane bumped across the runway. The view of the majestic pines outside the window reminded me of our strength. I'd come through a hell of a lot in the last few weeks since my alphas had come to me and woken me up to my true role. I'd faced challenge after challenge and won. No undead creeps were going to get the better of us now.

The jet rumbled to a stop. Kylie reached across the armrest to grip my hand. My best friend, who was as human as I'd used to think I was, had come to visit me with even less of an idea of the shifter community's turmoil than I'd had, but she was still here. Still supporting me even though she'd seen me at my most vicious. Still giving me that brilliant smile as her neon pink pixie cut shone under the overhead lights.

I didn't know whether I was more worried or grateful that she was here. But I wasn't pushing her away anymore.

West stood up first to open the plane door. The wolf shifter's dark green eyes blazed with concern for his kin and anger at the people who'd put them in danger. Seeing him like that, my heart squeezed.

The rest of us got up to follow West. "How many of your kin were heading to the estate?" Aaron asked Marco. The eagle shifter, alpha to the avian kin, had a habit of focusing in on the facts. Hearing his calm, warm voice always settled my nerves at least a little.

"There were seven of them using the house," Marco said. "The last I heard, three of them were on the run— one of them injured. We'll get the whole story now. They should have made it here before us." The jaguar shifter's usual mischievous gaze had darkened. He raked an anxious hand through his jagged black hair as he stalked down the aisle toward the exit.

Nate, the last of my alphas, stood back to let Kylie and me go ahead of him. He rested his strong hand on my shoulder. Tall and brawny as the grizzly bear he could shift into, he'd always had my back. But he was a total softie when we weren't under threat.

The early morning breeze rushed over me as we clattered down the steps. It was cool and thick with the smell of the pines. A high stone wall bordered the runway. I headed in the other direction, along a winding path through the trees, and discovered a house that matched the wall at the other end.

To call it a "house" was really underselling it. Kylie sucked in an awed breath when she saw it. The place was a mansion, no doubt about it. Three expansive floors encased in solid stone blocks, with an arch of dark hardwood over the heavy door.

Several of West's kin had come out to meet us. If we'd

been making our expected visit a day or two from now, there might have been a crowd. As it was, I couldn't help feeling grateful to see so few faces beaming at me in greeting. The canine shifters had always been welcoming to me—overwhelmingly so sometimes—but danger seemed to chase me wherever I went. I'd rather have fewer kin in the crossfire.

"Dragon shifter," they murmured first, with respectful bobs of their heads. The one who held himself with the most authority, one of West's lieutenants I guessed, turned to his alpha.

"Three feline kin arrived a couple hours ago. We offered them guest rooms, and the one who was wounded has been seen to."

Marco stepped up beside West. "Is she all right?"

The lieutenant—a coyote shifter by his scent—nodded quickly. "Her injuries were serious, but not fatal. She's sleeping now."

"And there's been no sign of vampires in this area—no word from any of the villages closer to New York City?" West asked.

"The settlement by the edge of New York City," the coyote shifter said with a grimace. "We got word that they'd scented vampires in the area not long after I last spoke with you. Then we lost contact. I sent a few of our people out there to check first hand."

West's jaw set. "You let me know as soon as you hear back."

One of the other canine kin, a fennec fox shifter with a narrow face and a shock of tawny hair, had zeroed his attention in on Kylie. "What's a *human* doing here?" he said in a needling voice.

I bristled. "She's my friend. Anywhere I go, she's welcome."

The fox shifter cocked his head. "I'm just saying, it seems like we've got major shifter business to take care of here, and I don't see—"

"*Felix*," West snapped. He pushed in front of us to glower at his underling, who stood a good half a foot shorter than the wolf shifter's lanky frame. West's teeth bared slightly. "As should be obvious, she's here with my permission."

The fox shifter's body had gone rigid. "Yes, sir. Of course. I wasn't thinking." He raised his chin high enough to show the pale length of his neck. I hadn't seen the gesture before, but there was something clearly apologetic about it.

Aaron had come up beside me. He leaned over to murmur by my ear. "Among canine shifters, exposing the throat is their most overt sign of submission."

West had already relaxed at the posturing. "All right," he said in his usual gruff voice. "Maybe try to do a little more thinking before you start shooting your mouth off next time? We *do* have a lot of important business to see to."

"And you'd better believe I'm going to help with that business," Kylie piped up. "Just wait. In a few days you'll be wondering why you don't have humans like me around all the time."

Felix raised a skeptical eyebrow, but he was smart

enough not to say anything with his alpha watching over him.

"Let's go in," West said. "We should talk with Marco's kin, find out exactly what happened."

The outside of the mansion had looked kind of hard and cold, but warmth washed over us as soon as we stepped inside. The walls were painted a subdued gold tone and thick rugs covered the floors. The front hall opened into a great room with a massive stone-lined fireplace that must be incredibly cozy in the winter. A hint of fresh-baked bread in the air caught my attention, and my stomach rumbled.

"I'll summon the feline kin," West's coyote shifter lieutenant said. His gaze slid to two of the other attendants. "Bring the alphas and our dragon shifter—*and* her friend—some breakfast."

West gave him a thin but approving smile. I sank onto one of the wool sofas, the cushion immediately enveloping me. This place was a lot like its master, I observed with a tickle of amusement. Tough and apparently impenetrable on the outside, but with unexpected pleasures if you made your way past those walls.

West was the only one of the four alphas I hadn't yet consummated my mate bond with. We'd had a tumultuous run of it over the last few weeks. He'd been skeptical of me from the start, but I'd thought he was softening toward me lately, at least a little. It was so hard to tell with him. But the moments of passion he'd allowed himself with me... My skin heated just remembering them, even with everything else on my mind.

Kylie sat down on the sofa at my left and Nate at my right. The bear shifter gave my knee a reassuring touch. Aaron took an armchair across from us, his golden Disney-prince hair gleaming in the dawn sunlight streaking through the picture window. West and Marco stayed on their feet. West stood stiffly, his arms folded over his chest, while Marco paced.

"This never should have happened," he muttered. "We barely scuffed up those vamps the other day. We *settled* things with the king. Why is he going to listen to a few mangy rogues whining to him anyway?"

He fell silent when breakfast appeared, buttered bread and jam and slices of fried ham that made my mouth water despite myself. I put together a quick sandwich to ease the pangs in my stomach.

I'd only gotten in a few bites when Marco's kin appeared, one of the figures familiar: Leonard the lion shifter, one of Marco's lieutenants, his round face split by jutting cheekbones. We'd had kind of an unfortunate first meeting. That was, he'd kidnapped me, thinking that was the easiest way to get me to his alpha.

Now, he looked even more down-beaten than when Marco had laid into him for that mistake. His eyes were hollowed and a slash of red ran across one of those high cheekbones where a wound was only just sealing. It looked like the scrape of a bullet. My gut clenched. I put my sandwich down on the coffee table.

"Look what the cat dragged in," Marco said, but he couldn't quite work a teasing lilt into his voice. He motioned Leonard and his companion, a stocky silver-hair woman who smelled like a lynx, to one of the other sofas. "Sit down before you talk. You've clearly done enough running for one night. We just need to know what happened at the house, and then you can get back to your napping."

Leonard dropped onto the sofa and leaned his head into his hands. He rubbed them up and down over his face.

"We had no idea they were coming," he said hoarsely. "We never keep watch that closely at the house—it's in the middle of the suburbs for Christ's sake. Not where you'd ever think... Right after sundown, they blasted down the door. At least ten of them, maybe fifteen. I couldn't have counted. They charged all through the place, spraying bullets. I barely pulled Lindy out of the way in time. Sandra and I carried her out to the car and got out of there. There wasn't anything else to do."

A chill ran over me. All of us around the great room had tensed. "Spraying bullets," I repeated. "They all had guns?" Some of the rogue shifters had fought us with pistols and rifles, going against one of the firmest shifter laws, but their resources when it came to human weaponry had seemed to be limited. I didn't know what restrictions vampires faced—or didn't.

Leonard shuddered. "They had *machine* guns, most of them. Pistol-sized, but still not anything I'd want to tangle with again. The bloodsuckers didn't even try to bite us. Knew they'd lose if it came to hand-to-hand fighting." His lips curled back. "Treaty-breakers *and* cowards."

Machine guns. Fucking hell. I saw the same horror echoed in all the alphas' expressions. How could we fight against an army of undead stocked up with military grade firearms?

"And they'll be dealt with as the treaty-breakers they are," Marco said, his voice taut. "I don't suppose they offered any clue as to what this surprise assault was prompted by? Blasting up our homes isn't one of their usual hobbies."

Leonard shook his head. "They didn't say anything at all. Just opened fire. And the other four in the house—they'd fallen before I even realized what was happening."

He faltered, his face crumpling. Marco stepped toward him.

"It isn't your fault," he said firmly. "You couldn't have expected an attack like that. And believe me, the bloodsuckers are going to pay."

"Is there anything else you saw or heard that might be useful to us, for fighting back?" Aaron asked.

"I... I can't think of anything. It all happened so fast." Leonard rubbed his face again. He was obviously exhausted.

"Sandra?" Marco said.

The lynx shifter looked equally worn-out—and shell shocked. She swayed a little on her cushion. "I did hear one of the vamps say something to one of the others," she said. "That—that they'd been hoping the shifters would take each other out, but handling it themselves was more fun." She winced at that last word.

My hackles rose. If there'd been a vampire in the room with us right then, I don't think anything could have restrained me from shooting my dragon talons from my hand and slicing its head straight off.

"They know we're getting stronger," I said. "Because I'm here. Because there's a dragon shifter to bring the kin together again." I inhaled sharply. "And I am going to do that. What Marco said is right. The vampires are going to pay, any way I can make them."

It was almost painful seeing the hope light behind the anguish in the lynx shifter's eyes. I'd better fulfill that promise, even if I wasn't entirely sure how yet.

"All right, you two," Marco said with a shooing motion. "You did what you could. You got out of there alive, and saved Lindy too. Now get your rest. We might need you by nightfall."

"What happens at nightfall?" Kylie asked as Leonard and Sandra headed back to their rooms.

"Not all the legends about vampires are true," West said. "But sunlight does burn them to a crisp. They can stroll around in the subway tunnels all right, but they can't make any attacks above ground until the sun goes back down."

"So we've got some time to decide our next steps." Nate leaned forward, running his hand over his thick chestnut-brown hair. "We should find out if there's been vampire activity near any of the other city centers where they have their clans. New York is the biggest one—what else is there?"

"Los Angeles," Aaron said. "Las Vegas. Chicago. And Atlanta. But they've got smaller pockets scattered through the smaller cities too."

"I don't understand," I burst out. "Why would they suddenly attack us like this? I know shifters and vampires aren't, like, friendly, but this… the comment Sandra said she overheard… It sounds like they hate us."

Marco grimaced. "There's no love lost between vamps and shifters, that's for sure. We keep the peace with our treaty rather than any affection on either side—the same as with the fae. It's always been easier for both of our peoples to keep to our own territories rather than get into some kind of war. I don't know why they've changed their minds about that."

"But it is war. No one could argue that. With guns that powerful…" I swallowed hard.

"We have our advantages," Nate said. "We can prepare by daylight, but we know how to fight in the dark as well."

"We won't be easy targets when they can't take us by surprise," West added.

I swiped my hand across my mouth. "Okay. So sunlight burns them up. What else can we use to our advantage? What else are they weak against?"

Marco raised an eyebrow as he looked at me. "After sunlight? I'd say what they're most afraid of is fire."

CHAPTER 2

Ren

The stone wall around the canine estate looked more than solid enough to keep out automatic gunfire. But of course that wouldn't help us if the vampires found their way over it. I bit my lip, considering it from where I stood in the front yard.

"What else do we have to worry about with vampires? They suck people's blood, they're stronger and faster than regular people—but not more than us—and it seems like they've got access to heavy artillery… Can they do the whole transforming into bats thing? Leap tall buildings with a single jump?"

Marco chuckled. "Shifters have the monopoly on animal transformations, princess, so no need to worry about that. And the bloodsuckers aren't Superman clones either. Their biggest advantage is that they're damned hard to kill, being already dead and all."

"Sunlight does the trick," West said, giving the sky a grim look. The sun was nearly at its noon peak, pouring summer heat over us. "And fire. A clean beheading. Not much else."

"Wooden stakes?" Kylie suggested, making a sweeping gesture with her arm as if brandishing one.

"I don't know anyone who's tried that," Nate said with a thoughtful frown.

Aaron would probably know—but he'd gotten a phone call five minutes ago and walked off around the house to talk undisturbed.

"Well, it's not as if we're likely to get close enough to stake any of them if they've got their guns blasting anyway," I said. "Fire will do the trick."

But my dragon fire would only help the kin here on the canine estate. My thoughts leapt to the shifter village we'd spent a couple nights in after my alphas had first found me. All the kin there who'd been so awed to meet me, to know the dragon shifter had finally returned...

Those small settlements didn't have big stone walls to halt bullets—and they didn't have any dragons to pour flames down on their attackers either. Protecting my people would be a hell of a lot easier if there were more shifters like me.

Maybe someday there would be. The thought gave me a twinge low in my belly. Once upon a time there'd been four dragon shifters—my mother and my sisters and me. If I fulfilled my bond with all of my alphas, then we could start thinking about raising children of our own.

But not now. Not into a world like this. I could fight for the shifters with everything I had as long as I only had myself to protect. It was saving me, trying to save my sisters, that had held my mother back when the rogues had first attacked all those years ago. She'd only been able to save me, and only by leaving the rest of her people behind.

Aaron emerged from the shadows around the house, fallen pine needles rustling under his feet. One look at his expression was enough to tell me he had more bad news.

"They hit one of yours too?" Marco said as the eagle shifter joined us.

Aaron nodded, his mouth set at a pained angle. "A small settlement just up the coast from L.A. The vampires surrounded the village so they could shoot at anyone who tried to fly out. A few were able to make it, but most... It was a slaughter. Alice is seeing that the survivors are looked after." He'd sent his sister back to the avian estate on the coast when the rest of us had headed to West's, so he'd have someone he completely trusted overseeing his own people.

My stomach turned. We'd had similar reports from the village of canine shifters near New York, an enclave of feline shifters not far from Atlanta, and a collective of Nate's disparate kin a few hours outside Las Vegas. The vampires had made their bloody intentions crystal clear. But they hadn't made any demands.

"And we still don't have any real idea what the vampires want?" I said.

"They want us all dead," West muttered. "That's obvious."

"I know that," I said, resisting the urge to snap at him.

"I mean *why*. If we knew why they've suddenly turned on us, we might be able to find some leverage we could use."

Nate made a discomforted sound. "As far as I can tell, the only 'leverage' the bloodsuckers are going to understand is being burned to a crisp. And I'm looking forward to seeing you teach them that lesson."

"If I were going to hazard a guess," Aaron said, "from what Marco's kin told us... They liked seeing us weakened without a dragon shifter. It reassured them when our kin started to pick at each other, new conflicts developing. They were hoping we'd keep heading down that road until we were right at each other's throats. But we've come back. As you said, we're getting stronger again, more unified."

He gave me a smile that was tight but genuine. "They may have realized this is their last chance to hit us before we're all the way to our former strength. And they got used to the idea that they might be rid of us. They didn't want to go back to how things were before, to having to work with us and make compromises."

"They can forget about compromising after the mess they've made of things around here," Marco said with a show of teeth.

But the vamps still had us at a disadvantage. I studied the wall again, thinking about all those villages that didn't have this kind of protection. "What exactly are the restrictions against shifters using weapons? Where do you draw the line?"

"We're not shooting back at them," West said.

"I *know*. Nothing that's intended as a weapon. But is

there a law against using *anything* other than our bodies in a fight?"

"What are you thinking, Ren?" Nate asked.

I motioned to the field beyond the estate's gate. "We want to burn the vamps to a crisp. Am I the only one allowed to do that, or can your kin fight with fire too?"

Aaron's gaze turned distant with thought. "Anything we'd hold and attack someone directly with, like a torch, would be forbidden. But there are other ways we could use fire."

"We still have the whole afternoon to prepare," I said. "Could you have your kin lay down a ring of flammable material around their villages—around the other estates, too—that they could easily light up if the vampires showed up? It'd be mostly for protection… but if they happened to set it off while some of the vamps were walking by, and those vamps happened to catch on fire, that'd get a pass, right?"

Marco's lips curled into a smirk. "I'm liking the way you think more and more every day, princess."

"It would unsettle them too," Nate said. "Easier for us to pick them off in the confusion. A good shove into the flames…" He wiped his palms together with a satisfied expression.

"Our kin will need to clear the vegetation from the area," Aaron said. "We don't want to end up burning a whole forest down. But there's time for that. It could at least hold the vampires back." Nodding to himself, he pulled out his phone. "I've got some more calls to make."

Kylie clapped her hands. "Well, *I'm* not bound by any shifter laws, am I? I wonder if I can scrounge up some kind of flame-thrower. I can definitely put you in touch with people who'll supply fuel on the down-low."

I smiled at my best friend. If she had a superpower, it was managing to make a friend or at least an acquaintance out of everyone she met, which was a lot of people. With all her connections, she could obtain just about anything you could possibly need, at least in the regular human part of the world. Which my alphas had first discovered back in New York when she'd gotten a lead on a puzzle the rest of us had drawn a blank on.

"I'll take those names," Nate said to Kylie.

"There," she said, reaching for her own phone. "You tell that Felix guy I'm already making myself more useful than he's doing, West."

The wolf shifter smirked at that comment. "I might do that right now." He waved a hand toward the house.

Someone must have been watching, because a minute later, several of West's attendants hurried out. The tawny-haired fennec fox shifter was in their midst. He glanced at Kylie as he hustled past. His expression switched to a glower when she gave him a thumbs-up and a broad grin.

"We need a ring of ground cleared just beyond the estate wall, at least ten feet wide," the canine alpha told his kin. "Any brush that'd hold a flame, collect it for us to lay down the middle. We can douse it with gasoline for good measure."

"Hold on," I said as they headed for the gate. "You don't need that here. *I'm* here."

West gave me a baleful look. "You're just one dragon, Sparks, in case you forgot. A dragon who can only manage to stay a dragon maybe a half hour if you're lucky. If the vamps turn up here, we'll have to hold them off for the whole night."

"It's not going to take me the whole night to fry them," I retorted. "It's not like I'm going to toast one and then take a ten-minute whirl around the estate before I get around to the next."

"And if they come in waves? If you miss some before you run out of juice?"

I crossed my arm over my chest. "I can pace myself. And I've shifted twice in the same day before. Night shouldn't be any different."

He sighed. "Look, Sparks, it seems to me we're better off having the extra protection just in case one dragon isn't enough to save the day. These are my people here, and I'll be damned if I don't do everything I can to protect them. Unless you have some brilliant plan for destroying every vampire out there before the sun even goes down?"

He had a point. I knew he had a point. It was just that the way he made that point niggled at me. "No," I admitted. "I don't. Believe me, if I did, I wouldn't be keeping quiet about it."

"Oh, believe *me*, I know that," West said with a glint in his eyes. Before I could decide whether it was teasing or hostile, another thought struck me.

"*Could* we take the battle to the vampires?" I asked. "They're totally vulnerable during the day, right? If we found their hideouts and—"

Marco, who'd stayed near us, started shaking his head. "One compliment I'll willingly give the bloodsuckers—they're nothing if not painstaking when it comes to being careful with their daytime routines. They'll be behind about twenty locked doors in some deep dark basement—dozens of deep dark basements, all across those cities. And we don't even know which basements. I suppose if we burned the entire city to the ground..."

I exhaled sharply. "I get it. No luck there. Maybe we need to find ourselves some secret basements to hide out in too."

"If things get desperate, I get the impression your friend might have some ideas on that score," Marco said, looking amused.

Yeah, Kylie probably knew at least a handful of abandoned buildings we could hole up in for a while. But that would only help us until the vampires found us again. We needed to convince them it was too much trouble trying to exterminate us—or we needed to exterminate them while they tried.

The gate squeaked open again. Felix came in, holding up a young man so wobbly and bloody it looked like he'd have fallen over without the help. My heart leapt into my throat.

Marco's eyes widened. "Timothy," he said, striding over.

The injured shifter gave the feline alpha a hazy look.

"He just stumbled over to where we were working," Felix said. "He hasn't said anything. I'm not sure he even can."

"Get him inside," West said. "Quickly. He needs rest and someone to look at those wounds."

Marco took Timothy's other arm. He and Felix led the poor guy into the estate house together. I hurried after them, my heart thudding. Had the vampires made another attack? Just now, in the middle of the day? That shouldn't even be possible.

Timothy's feet started to drag on the floor. Marco flinched at the sound and hefted him higher. "We've got you. Just a little farther."

"Over here," West said, opening a door just down the hall from the great room. An office, from the looks of it, with two walls of built-in bookshelves, a desk, an armchair—and a sofa, where Marco and Felix laid the feline shifter down.

Timothy shuddered and coughed. "Water!" Marco snapped. Felix went running. The jaguar shifter knelt beside his fallen kin.

Timothy hadn't been shot—or at least, if he had, those weren't the wounds currently bleeding. A deep gouge across the side of his ribs was slowly shrinking. A large chunk of hair had been scraped off his scalp. I cringed inside as I noted each injury. What had happened to him?

He obviously couldn't tell us yet.

"I can call one of my kin to—" West began.

Marco cut him off with a jerk of his hand. "I'll do it. He's my responsibility."

He flicked a jaguar claw from one index finger and dug it into the flesh of his wrist. I winced outright at the sudden stream of blood. Jaw clenched, Marco let some trickle over Timothy's side and then his head, combining the healing power of his healthy body with his underling's best efforts. Then he pressed his opposite palm to his wrist to encourage his own cut to heal.

Timothy murmured, his limbs relaxing into the couch. His eyelids fluttered. Felix reappeared clutching a glass of water. "Thank you," Marco said, accepting it. He returned to his kin and held the glass to Timothy's lips.

The feline shifter managed a couple of swallows. He exhaled a relieved breath. Marco turned to set the glass on the side table, and Timothy's hand shot out to grasp the front of his alpha's shirt.

"Alpha," he rasped.

"Hey," Marco said, putting his hand over Timothy's. "You need to recover. It's a miracle you managed to escape them at all." He glanced up at me. "He's one of the missing four from my New York house."

He shouldn't know much more than Leonard and Sandra had, then. But Timothy yanked on Marco's shirt again. "No," he said. "Didn't escape. They sent me. I'm a message."

Beside me, West stiffened. Marco's gaze sharpened. "What's the message, Timothy?"

"Tonight," the injured shifter choked out. "The king will parlay with you tonight, at full-dark, by the Marveille crossroads."

CHAPTER 3

Nate

I ROUNDED a corner in the canine estate's halls a little too quickly and bumped shoulders with one of West's kin. The jackal shifter took one look at my face and cowered backward. His chin twitched upward with that instinctive reaction all the canines had to show their throats when avoiding a fight. "My apologies, alpha. I promise to be more careful."

Shit. I must look something fierce for him to react like that. I willed my expression as calm as I could manage—which probably wasn't all that much, consider the amount of the frustration churning inside me. "It's all right," I said. "I bumped into *you*. No offense taken."

He didn't look completely convinced. As he darted off, I forced myself to stay in place, leaning back against the wall. I swiped my hand over my face as if I could rub the tension out of it.

I'd been prowling the estate for the better part of an hour, and I didn't think I'd burnt off any of that frustrated energy. I'd already made all the calls I could to my lieutenants and other kin. Every settlement within half a night's drive of any vampire stronghold was already making preparations to fend off their gunfire with fire of our own.

Normally I'd have been flying out there to join them, to stand on the front lines. But Ren needed me. Our bond was only just solidified. She was still so new to her role as dragon shifter.

And even if she could have spared me for the night, we were meant to parlay with the vampire king just after nightfall not far from here.

Maybe this whole mess would be settled then. But after hearing about the mass murders the vamps had already committed against my kin and the other alphas'... I wasn't counting on it. I sure as hell wasn't in a compromising mood.

But lumbering around the house like a rampaging grizzly in a man's body obviously wasn't helping anything. I dragged in a breath and pushed myself off the wall. I should probably try to get in some sleep before it was time to head out. We might have a very long night ahead of us.

I headed toward the south end of the third floor, where the main bedrooms were, but my restless feet took me right past the door to my own suite. I stopped in front of Ren's. She'd gone up here after lunch to prepare herself for the night ahead. Maybe she'd appreciate the company.

I eased open the door and found myself looking at my mate's back where she was poised on the sitting room floor. She had her legs crossed and her hands resting on her knees, her head tipped slightly back, her dark brown hair cascading past her shoulders. I loomed high enough over her to see her eyes were closed.

Whatever zone she was trying to get into, I didn't want to disturb her. I stepped backward, but the door hinges squeaked at my tug. Ren's eyes popped open with a jump of her shoulders.

"Sorry," I said, holding up my hands. "I didn't mean to interrupt."

She groaned and flopped down on her back. "It's okay. I'm not sure I was getting much of anywhere anyway."

She seemed to mean that as an invitation. I hunkered down on the floor beside my mate. "Where were you trying to get?"

Ren squirmed a little closer to me, and I was more than happy to loop my arm across her waist as she rested her head against my leg. Just that simple touch eased the tension in me so much more than anything else I'd tried. Maybe I hadn't come in here just for her comfort but for my own as well.

"I was hoping practicing some meditation might help me extend my shifting ability," she said. "I want to be able to hold the shift longer. Long enough to deal with every single vampire we need to fight."

"Hopefully we won't be fighting any of them, if we can settle things with the parlay."

She gave a dismissive-sounding snort, which was

about the way I felt about that possibility too. "I have to be ready."

"You've been picking up the skill really quickly, you know," I said, stroking my thumb over her side. She was wearing the same T-shirt she'd had on this morning, but the warmth of her skin radiated through the soft fabric. "It's not exactly the same situation, but for kids, when they're first learning, it usually takes them a few years from when they can manage their first partial shift to reach a full shift. And then it's several more years before any of us gets to the point that we can hold our animal form nearly indefinitely. You got through the first stage in just a few days."

"Because I'm not a kid," Ren said. "Because I should have been doing it all along. But the endurance part is taking a lot longer. I don't have several years. I don't even have several days. The vampires have already hurt us so much more than the rogues managed to."

"They're nasty, but they're smart," I said. "And organized, and disciplined. Things the rogues definitely weren't, or they wouldn't have rejected the kin groups in the first place. But we can still beat the bloodsuckers. You're doing everything you can. The vampires are *afraid* of you, you know. That's why they're attacking now. They know that with every day you're making the entire shifter community stronger and stronger."

"And I'm going to keep doing that," Ren said. I loved seeing that fiery determination light in her amber eyes.

Then she yawned, covering her face with her arm to try to hide it.

"Okay," I said. "I think both of us need some rest to

be ready for tonight. You can meditate more in your sleep."

"I don't think it works like that," Ren muttered. I got up, sweeping her into my arms, and a squeak of protest slipped from her lips. "Nate! I can make it from here to the bed."

"But this is more fun," I said.

She muttered a little more, but she also nestled her head against my shoulder. I tucked my chin over her hair as I carried her to the bed. My mate was strong, yes, but it didn't hurt her to let the rest of us be strong for her every now and then.

I climbed onto the bed and lay down with her, sharing a pillow. Ren ruffled my hair. "My big strong bear," she said as if she'd read my thoughts, with so much affection my heart thumped happily. I bent my head to kiss her. She slid her arm behind my neck as she kissed me back, pulling me even closer against her, and suddenly sleep was the last thing on my mind.

My hand skimmed down her side to her hip and back up to cup her breast. Ren's breath stuttered against my mouth. She kissed me harder as I drew her nipple to a stiff peak, a whimper working its way from her throat. When she drew back, her cheeks were flushed and her eyes sparkling.

"We should get that rest," she said. "But maybe if we're *really* quick, there's room for a little more fun first?"

I laughed. "I can't say no to that." Then I rolled right onto her, intent on turning that whimper into a moan.

～

Ren

Kylie was exactly where Aaron had told me he'd last seen her, in a small lounge room just off the main hall. She grinned when I came in, unfolding her petite body from her armchair. "Ren!" Then her expression turned abruptly serious. "Is it time for you to leave already?"

I shook my head, sitting down on the chair beside hers. "We've got about another hour. I've just been thinking..." I paused, trying to figure out the best way to approach this subject. The last thing I wanted was my best friend thinking I was trying to ditch her. But I wasn't going to feel okay unless we had this one last conversation.

"Thinking what?" Kylie prodded, watching me.

I met her gaze, hoping she could read the emotion in mine. "You know how much I appreciate having you here. How glad I've been to have you on my side for the whole time we've been friends. So I promise you I'm not saying this because of what I *want*. But because you matter so much to me, I have to ask, now that things have gotten even more dangerous—are you sure you want to stay here?"

Kylie gave me a wry smile. "Where else would I go?"

"Back to your old life, I guess," I said. "You have our apartment—I can keep paying my share of the rent, and hopefully I'll be able to visit lots. You have your job. The vampires won't hassle you there. But as long as you're here with the shifters... I don't think it'll matter that you're not one too. They're not being careful with their bullets."

"Okay," Kylie said. "I get why you're worried. I'm not exactly feeling super keen about taking on gun-toting vampires either. But can I ask you something, and you answer totally honestly?"

"Of course," I said.

She tipped her head, studying my expression even more carefully now. "If you could have your life be any way you wanted right now, just the most perfect possible situation, what would that look like?"

God, what a question. Just the idea of being able to shed all this conflict made my heart swell and ache at the same time. I let my mind drift into that imaginary scenario. What would it look like if I could have everything I wanted? I'd promised her total honesty.

"I'd be living with all four of the guys, everyone happy and getting along, no more doubts between us. Going from estate to estate and to different towns, I guess, helping solve whatever little squabbles came up. And you'd be there, of course. So we could hang out and have some girl time whenever I didn't have other stuff to take care of."

I focused on her again. "But I have no idea when—if —I'll get to that point. And that's just what *I'd* want. You've got a life too. I wouldn't want you sticking around if you'd be happier living a normal life. One where there weren't vampires taking shots at us and who knows what else in the future."

Kylie beamed back at me as if no possible future horror could faze her at all. "What's so great about normal?" she said. "I just wanted to know where I'd fit in when you're not worrying about my safety. Because this is exactly where I want to be too. If you're happy to have me sticking around, if I can do some kind of job here instead of that crappy one back in NYC, I'm totally in. Sure, hanging out with shifters can be kind of scary, but it's also pretty amazing."

I swallowed hard, so much joy bubbling up inside me that I didn't know what to do with it. "You're sure?" I said. "Really, *really* sure?"

Kylie laughed. "I've had a lot of time to think about it in the last couple days, you know. And there really hasn't been even one moment where I wished I hadn't come out here. So you're meant to be queen of all shifters—I'm pretty sure I'm meant to be your right-hand girl. I might not have any paranormal destiny, but it feels fated to me."

The emotion overwhelmed me. Talking didn't seem like enough. I hopped up and grabbed my best friend in a hug. She squeezed me back. "There," she said. "I'm glad we got that settled. Once and for all? You really need to stop trying to protect me. I'm a big girl."

"I know," I said. "I promise, this is the last time I'll bring it up. I just wanted to be completely sure. If something happened to you and I thought you'd only been there for my sake..."

"Nope," Kylie said. "I'm one hundred percent in this for me too. I mean, just look at these digs." She gestured to the room around her with a mischievous glint in her eyes. But when she turned back to me she'd gone a bit serious again. "I know what I'm getting into here, Ren. And I'm ready for it."

I exhaled and gave her a crooked smile. "Good. I really hope that I am too. Come on, we'd better grab some dinner. I'd rather not be fighting vamps on an empty stomach."

CHAPTER 4

Ren

"Does this crossroads give them any kind of an advantage if this comes down to a fight?" I asked West. I was sitting next to him in the jeep he'd picked from the assorted vehicles on his estate.

He'd driven quickly most of the way out here, but the last twenty miles we were taking slow and wary. The vibration of the engine thrummed through the seat beneath me. A matching rumble carried through the air from the cars ahead of and behind us.

"Immediately around the crossroads the terrain is pretty open," West said without taking his eyes off the road. "Not much shelter for us. I'd prefer surroundings like what we have right here if I had the choice."

He nodded to the pine forests looming on either side of the narrow highway. In the deepening night, the dark points of the treetops cut into the shadowy blue of the clouded sky. The moon still gleamed faintly through a thinner patch of haze.

One of his kin in the back had been in communication with the scouts West had sent ahead earlier. "Rayanne says there's at least fifty of the vamps gathered now," he said, a worried note in his voice.

West's jaw tightened. The other alphas had come too, of course, in other cars, and a few dozen of West's kin as well in case we needed back-up. But...

"If fifty vamps means fifty guns, we won't stand much of a chance," I said.

"No kidding, Sparks," West said. "Do you want to head back?"

I couldn't tell if he meant the question seriously or as a jab. "Is that really an option?" I said.

He gave a choked laugh. "I guess that depends on how much diplomacy matters to you."

"I'm not thinking about diplomacy. I'm thinking about not getting us killed."

"Believe me, that's at the top of my priority list too. Any brilliant suggestions for how to weight the odds?"

They might be calling us to this parlay to try to slaughter me and the alphas the way the rogues had failed to. Or they might honestly be willing to negotiate some kind of peace. Ha. On the other hand, if we *didn't* show up, we were pretty much ensuring that they'd immediately attack the shifter community again. Horrible situation or awful situation. I'll take neither, please!

Of course, *that* definitely wasn't an option. I sighed.

"I didn't even know vampires existed a month ago. Shouldn't you have a better idea than I do?"

"I don't think you'd like the idea I'm having," West muttered.

What the hell was that supposed to mean?

Just then, the phone's alert went off again. The guy in the back made a disgruntled sound. "Another truck full of the bloodsuckers showed up. And they're fanning out around the crossroads. Blending into the darkness like they do, but our people can scent them. It looks like they're planning on having us surrounded after we arrive."

That didn't sound like preparation for an honest conversation. West and I exchanged a glance. His expression had gone even grimmer.

"We can't meet them like that," I said, braced for another snarky comment.

But the wolf shifter nodded. "No. There are risks and then there's insanity. Bertrand, is there anywhere decent to park between here and there?"

His lieutenant scanned the area on a phone map. "There's an old gas station a couple miles down the road. Out of business, so there won't be anyone there, and the lot looks a decent size."

"That's our place, then. Tell the other cars to convene there."

"And then what?" I asked.

West's smile was still grim. "Then we tell the vampires we've met them close enough to halfway, and if they want us, they can come to us, on ground *we* chose.

And if they try any funny business while they're arriving, we deal with them then."

"The guns," one of the guys in the back said, and cut himself off with a swipe across his mouth as if worried he sounded too nervous.

"If the vamps start firing, we should get out of there," I said. "Everyone in the cars, head back to the estate. Tell them that too."

The second I stopped speaking, I wondered if I'd crossed a line, giving orders to West's kin. But he didn't comment. I guessed that meant he agreed with the plan. He'd pressed his foot to the gas, speeding up so we'd reach our new destination sooner. The sky was almost fully black now.

"I'll cover everyone," I added. "Lay down some fire of my own to hold them off while the rest of you are getting away."

West's gaze shot to me again. "Don't be stupid, Ren. You'll need to get out of there too. You're the last one we can afford to lose."

"I'm the most likely one to make sure we don't lose anyone," I said. "I can dodge a few bullets."

"You haven't faced guns like this before."

He wasn't entirely wrong. But my mind slid back to Fisher, the guy I'd stolen for in exchange for food and shelter alongside a bunch of other street kids when I'd been fending for myself after Mom had disappeared. To the revolver he'd always kept shoved in the back of his jeans. To the guns I'd caught glimpses of on some of his colleagues when they'd come to collect.

"You don't know what I've seen before this. I'd bet I've seen more guns than you have."

"That doesn't mean you should throw yourself at them," West snapped.

I tensed, but he looked immediately chagrined. Because he regretted saying that to me or he regretted saying it that way in front of his kin? Who knew? But I felt, underneath the tense anticipation coiled through his body, a quiver of concern.

Maybe he didn't want to put all his faith in me to save his kin. Maybe he didn't trust my ideas. But whatever the case, he was also at least a little bit worried about *me*.

The retort that had been on my tongue wisped away. "I'm not looking to get shot," I said, my voice softening. "I'll only do what I have to, to make sure we all get out. And all of us includes me."

"Well, I'm not leaving until you're leaving," West said —gruffly, but even though I wouldn't have expected anything else, hearing him say it brought a heady flutter into my chest. Like when he'd kissed me last night, with a new tenderness I hoped I'd get to experience again.

But not now, obviously. The arched beams of the gas station sign came into view up ahead. The truck and the sedan ahead of us turned in, and West followed them.

We parked along the edge of the abandoned lot. With a rev of an engine, any of the cars should be able to leap the shoulder back onto the road if we needed to make a hasty exit.

Dry leaves that must have been left over from last fall crunched under my feet when I stepped out. The sign overhead creaked as the wind swung it on its chains. The pumps must have been completely dry—not even the faintest tang of gasoline reached my sharp shifter nose. Only the pine scent of the forest, like back at West's estate, with an added edge of rusting metal.

"Give me the phone," West said, holding out his hand. His lieutenant handed it over. As the rest of our contingent spilled out of their vehicles, the canine alpha called up one of his scouts.

"Rayanne. Slight change of plans. The vamps can meet us at a gas station six miles down the highway from that crossroads. You tell them that from as far of a distance as you can manage, and then hop on that motorcycle of yours and come join us. I don't want them taking any 'disappointment' out on you."

The other alphas had ambled over to join us. "Let's see if they still want to play ball when we're wise to their tricks," Marco said with a fierce smirk.

"I'd imagine they'll realize why we're changing the plan," Aaron said. "If they believe they have anything to gain from coming to a compromise at all, they'll accept. If violence was their only goal..." His jaw set. He glanced down the highway as if we might see the vampires heading our way already.

They might still come then. With guns in hand, ready to open fire.

The scout called back in. West brought the phone to his ear, said a few encouraging words, and then glanced around at us.

"They appear to have agreed to meet us here. They're on the move now. Be ready."

"Where do you want all of us stationed, sir?" Bertrand asked.

"We don't want to give them a reason to think we're here anything but peacefully," Aaron said. "That'll end this parlay before it even starts."

"Even when they came out in full force against us already," Nate muttered. He stepped closer to me. "Let them just try to complain."

"No, the eagle shifter is right," West said. He nodded to his kin. "Spread out into the woods, but stay on our side of the lot. Just far enough back that they won't be able to see you. Vamps can't rely on smell. But I want you close enough to engage if you need to—or jump into those cars and get out of here if it comes to that. You know the signals."

Except for a few who continued to flank us, the rest of the canine shifters faded back into the forest beside the gas station.

Lights glowed in the distance down the highway. My shoulders tensed. Here were the bloodsuckers.

"I should shift now," I said. "So I'm ready. The second I see one gun, I'm blasting them all. If they actually negotiate, you guys have a better idea than I do what the treaty says anyway. Any arguments there?"

None of the alphas gave me one. "Just be careful," Aaron said.

Marco shot me a grin. "They're the ones who'll need to be careful with our Princess of Flames on the prowl."

They kept watching the road while I peeled off my clothes. When the first trucks were close enough that I could make out the shape of them behind their headlights, I knelt on the ground and beckoned the shift through my body.

It was a pleasure, getting to shift at a natural pace rather than rushing into it as quickly as I could force the change. My muscles stretched and tingled rather than aching. The scales rippled over my skin with a giddy shiver. My wings swept out from my back, sending a rush of anticipation through my nerves. I loomed over the cars, fire already prickling at the base of my dragon's throat.

I didn't think I'd have any use for my truth-seeking flames tonight. If the vampires who'd slaughtered our kin took one step wrong, I was turning them into instant barbeque. It wouldn't solve the problem of all the other vampire groups out there, but at least it'd knock down their numbers a little. And be plenty satisfying at the same time.

The trucks, small delivery ones with no windows on the bulky back compartments, slid into the lot, staying on the opposite side from us. I kept my dragon eyes trained on the windshields, the doors, for any hint of a figure raising a gun.

A slim, dapper-looking man stepped out of the cab of the middle truck. His hair was pure black and his eyes glinted with some semblance of life, but his skin was deathly pale. A sour smell reached my nostrils.

The stench of the undead, that only our sensitive shifter noses could pick up. Their human victims never realized.

This guy was clearly the king. He strode into the middle of the lot, past the vacant pumps, as if he wasn't worried for himself at all. His gaze didn't even flicker my way, even though there was no way he could have missed the massive dragon watching him. Nine of his people gathered behind him, standing guard. The others stayed in the trucks.

"We've come to your parlay," West said. He and the other shifters were poised by the first of our cars, ready to use it as a shield. "Maybe you'd like to explain why your people attacked so many of ours last night?"

The vampire king smiled thinly. "That was a demonstration. To provide context for this talk."

"That context meant more than a hundred deaths among our kin," Nate said, his voice almost a growl.

The king looked at him blandly. "And now you know how serious I am. But no one else *needs* to die."

"Wonderful," Marco said. "We're duly informed of your seriousness. How about you get on with the actual reason you're here?"

"This is entirely your fault," the vampire king said in a haughty tone. "We all know the space for the supernatural kind in the modern world is dwindling. We vampires have learned how to adapt, how to blend in among the humans so that they don't discover us. But you shifters." A sneer crept into his voice. "Like the animals you transform into, you let your baser instincts overcome common sense. You run around without control. You can't stick to a human form."

"We take care of any troubles caused by our own kind," Aaron said.

"Not well enough. You can't even control your own kind enough to stop them from turning against you. I've heard all about the chaos of your community from shifters who've already attacked you more than once and gotten away." He let out a faint huff. "You're careless, and eventually you're going to be found out. And then the humans will be on the hunt for the rest of us too. None of us is safe while you continue giving into those animal impulses."

"We need to shift just like you need to drink blood," West said tightly. "You don't see us trying to stop you from eating."

"We don't need to run around in the open with our fangs out to eat," the king retorted. He slapped his hands together. "From my view, it would be better if we were rid of all of you. But I'm willing to consider an alternative. We have identified a few isolated areas of the country humans find so unpleasant they rarely travel there. You will stay there, and never cross those boundaries—and then you may live."

Did he really think we'd agree to that? Move the entire shifter community to some inhospitable zones— and what, with the vampires guarding us like refugee camps, making sure we never ventured out? I bared my teeth.

"You have to know that's a completely unreasonable suggestion," Aaron said.

Marco chuckled dryly. "We're not going to uproot all of our kin just so you can indulge your paranoia. What else have you got? We might be willing to work with you —if you're actually working *with* us and not just trying to herd us into a pen."

The king's posture shifted. I felt it from him then, before he'd even opened his mouth—he'd been playing the part of negotiating, but he'd never really expected us to accept. And he'd just checked out of the discussion completely.

Checked out to give himself over to the other purpose of this meeting.

A roar of warning broke from my throat just as a flood of vampires burst from the backs of the trucks.

CHAPTER 5

Ren

FIRE RUSHED up my throat after my roar. I'd have fried the vampire king into cinders just like that if he hadn't moved so fast. The boss bloodsucker leapt into the shadows around the old gas pumps and vanished. Apparently the vamps couldn't just blend into the darkness—they could disappear right into it too.

I didn't have time to figure out if I could chase him through the shadows. Dozens of vampire soldiers were charging forward to take his place, swinging the guns they must have had stashed in the trucks to aim at me and my alphas.

Fuck that. I spewed out the flames crackling at the back of my mouth with a sharp heave of breath. My dragon fire washed over the bloodsuckers in a wave. Every vampire body it touched burst into cinders.

Several shots rattled out over the hiss of the flames. A

bullet caught my shoulder with a tiny burst of pain. Not enough to slow me down. With a whip of my head and a fresh spurt of fire, those guns turned into so much misshapen garbage.

I sprang forward into the heap of ashen dust I'd created, readying for another blast. A bunch of the vampires had gotten smart, racing for the tree line at the edge of the lot. My next outpouring of fire caught the stragglers, but more than I liked escaped into the shelter of the trees where I'd have to take them down one by one.

Shots rang out and snarls carried from the forest. The shifters who'd come as our defenders must be circling around the lot to hold off the vampire attackers.

"Into the cars!" Nate was shouting. "The parlay is done."

West's voice, harsh with anger, broke through the bear shifter's. "Everyone, let's get out of here, *now*. Do not engage unless you have to."

The vampires who'd walked to meet us with their king unarmed had run for their own trucks. To grab more guns, I'd bet. They could forget that—and forget driving the trucks as well. I wasn't letting them give chase once we got on the road.

I rained fire down on the fronts of the vehicles, melting the metal hoods and the engine workings underneath into twisted blobs. The windshields shattered with the heat. A few of the vampires around back ducked from behind the cargo areas, guns in hand. I leapt higher into the air, summoning another stream of fire.

I didn't catch one of them in time. The automatic gun

thundered, its spray of bullets searing across my hind legs and thigh. I shrieked more in rage than pain and pelted the vamp with flames. In an instant, he and his gun were a molten lump.

More gunfire was still going off amid the trees. Ignoring the stinging ache radiating through my legs, I took off toward the forest. Some of the shifters were dashing to our cars, but others were still wrestling with the vampires, trying to cover their kin's escape.

A black wolf slashed open one vamp's neck, and the bloodsucker crumpled into a healing stasis. Two foxes, a red one and a tawny one with huge ears I guessed was Felix, sank their teeth into another vampire's legs at the same time and yanked. The vamp tumbled, and Felix was at his throat a second later.

The trees made it harder for the vamps to get a clear shot with their guns, but that didn't stop them from using their weapons. Bullets thunked into tree trunks and bark sprayed. A coyote stumbled and fell as the hail of bullets caught it across the chest. Marco's lion lieutenant, who'd joined us for the parlay, sprang at a bloodsucker and bashed the woman's head into a jutting root. Before he could wheel, another vamp had leapt from behind a tree and started shooting.

Blood burst from wounds down Leonard's side. I caught the vamp with a spurt of fire. A couple of canine shifters ran to grab the lion shifter as he crumpled, transforming back into human form. They hefted their injured ally up to carry him to the waiting cars.

I fried another two vampires. Between the pain spreading from my own wounds and the energy I'd expelled already, my dragon body was starting to prickle. I wasn't going to be able to hold the shift much longer.

Lights glowed across our end of the parking lot. Engines rumbled as the canine kin waited for the last few stragglers to make it to the vehicles. A couple cars had already pulled away. As the rest of the fighting shifters broke from the trees to make an escape, the remaining vampires pushed to the edge of the forest where they could more easily pick us off.

Not if I had anything to say about it. I dove, blazing a line of fire along the edge of the lot. In his wolf form, West wove among the fleeing shifters, urging them on toward the cars. Nate's bear charged at the vampires that were trying to dodge my flames. At the other end of the lot, Aaron and Marco had tackled the last of the vamps by the trucks.

My flames flickered out. I wrenched at my chest, trying to produce more, but my lungs stuttered. In that moment, one of the vampires sprang forward and pulled his trigger with his gun pointing straight at Nate's back.

West shoved the bear shifter to the side, but his wolf was barely big enough to jostle the much bigger animal. The bullets clipped the grizzly's head and streaked down his side. Nate groaned, spinning around but already swaying.

No! Panic knifed through me, twisting my gut. The fury that followed it blazed up so fast and hard my vision hazed white.

Not my mate. These undead monsters were *not* taking him from me.

More fire than I'd have thought I'd had in me—more

fire than I'd have imagined I could ever have summoned —ripped up from my lungs. It scorched my throat and singed my own teeth. I expelled it all with a scream of anger.

The rush of flames crashed into the vampires at the edge of the forest, searing through all of them before they could so much as flinch. It seared up the trees too. Up the trunks, blackening the bark and biting into the wood beneath. Flickering into the leaves, filling the air with smoke. The rising wind whipped it into a fury to match my own.

A fury I couldn't control. The fire surged from tree to tree, burning the rest of the vampires up or sending them running into the shadows. But it didn't stop. It crackled on, devouring all the vegetation in its path.

I hit the ground. My human legs sagged as I shifted. Blood streaked down my pale skin from the bullets I'd taken.

Aaron rushed to my side. West and Marco had shifted back into human form too, hauling Nate into the back of one of our vans. The bear shifter's head drooped in West's grasp, his skin waxen. A dribble of blood spotted the pavement along their path.

"He's alive," Aaron said, but I thought I heard an unspoken *for now* in there. My raw throat squeezed shut. I stumbled upright at the eagle shifter's tug. He pulled my arm across his shoulders and looped his around my waist.

The fire blazed on through the forest, its heat wafting over us. A shudder passed through me.

"I started a whole forest fire."

"There's nothing we can do about it now," Aaron said. "As soon as we're on the road, I'll call the closest fire department. They'll know what steps to take."

He started to lead me to one of the other cars, but I shook my head. "I want to be with Nate. I *need* to be with Nate."

Aaron looked as if he might have argued, but then he changed his mind. "All right. But someone has to tend to you too."

I hobbled with him to the van. A couple of kin were already bent over Nate's prone body, sharing blood and digging out the bullets. "Ren," West said hoarsely, but Aaron waved him away.

"We should get back to our cars. Get everyone out of here before any more vamps show up."

"Right." West shook off his momentary hesitation and bellowed down the end of the lot. "Everyone! Move out!"

I half scrambled, half dragged myself onto the van bed next to Nate. Another canine shifter leapt to see to my wounds. I closed my eyes, tuning out his attentions and pressing my face to my mate's shoulder. The glimpse I'd gotten of Nate's torn-up torso was more than I ever wanted to see again.

Nate's chest still rose and fell with steady if shallow breaths. I longed to squirm closer, to hear the thump of his heart in his chest, but I was afraid to disturb the wounds that hadn't yet closed. Instead I nestled as close to him as I dared, willing with every shred of my soul for him to heal. For him to be okay.

The van's engine rumbled, but the roar of the forest fire carried over it. Flames danced behind my eyelids as the wheels lurched over the uneven ground to the highway.

Not all of the destruction here was the vampires' doing. In that moment when I'd seen my mate fall, I hadn't been thinking at all, only acting. A mindless animal, like the vampire king had said. It wasn't just Nate who might die because of this battle tonight. And if any innocent people did, those deaths would be on *my* conscience.

As we roared down the highway toward the canine estate, I wasn't sure which potential tragedy made my heart ache harder.

CHAPTER 6

Aaron

Dawn light was only just starting to seep through the trees beyond my bedroom window when I pushed myself out of bed, but I wasn't getting much sleep there anyway. Bleary-eyed but with humming nerves, I found myself wandering down the hall to the healer's dormitory.

The room held several cots, but right now only two were occupied. The other shifters injured in last night's battle must have recovered enough to return to their own quarters.

Nate was still sprawled on his cot like he had been when I'd left the room a few hours ago. The healers who'd attended to my fellow alpha were leaving him be for now. They'd bandaged his wounds, and blood hadn't seeped through the white gauze, so I could assume at least that they weren't bleeding anymore. He was still breathing. He just hadn't woken up.

Serenity was curled up on top of the covers of the bed next to his, her eyes finally closed. Even asleep, her face looked tense. She'd been afraid of disturbing Nate but unwilling to return to her own room last night, despite the healers' cajoling. Her own wounds had closed, only angry pink marks still dotting her pale legs. Soon they'd fade too, like all the other injuries she'd taken in her first few weeks as our dragon shifter.

What an introduction to the shifter community she'd had. Every time I thought the worst was over, the world upped the ante on us all over again.

I didn't want to wake her. There wasn't anything I could do for Nate. I'd at least seen he was still alive. But I couldn't quite convince my feet to carry me back to my own room. All that waited for me there was more restless dozing.

The door to the healer's dorm clicked open. Marco slunk in, looking as weary as I felt. He came to a stop beside me.

"No change?"

"Not for the worse, at least," I said.

"Small blessings." The jaguar shifter's lips curled as if he couldn't decide whether to smile or grimace and had ended up halfway in between. "What the hell are we going to do without the bear's strength?"

"We'd lose a lot more than that if we lost him."

"That's true," Marco agreed. The feline alpha must have sensed as much as I did that in a lot of ways Nate was the glue that had held our quartet of clashing personalities together—with his strength, but also that easy warmth he always seemed to radiate, unless you gave him a good reason to get angry. It was hard to squabble all that much when he was around.

We hadn't even come together properly yet, not with West still dangling the possibility of eschewing the mating alliance altogether. I'd thought the canine alpha was starting to come around, but what would happen if Nate died? How united would we be then? The young man he'd have been training to take the alpha position after him wouldn't be of age yet. Either the disparate kin would fall into fighting over the rulership, or Serenity would be left without another mate.

If we lost Nate, the vampires might have won already, without even one more drop of blood shed.

"Have you seen West this morning?" I asked Marco.

He nodded. "Wolf boy is prowling around the common rooms snapping at anyone he doesn't like the look of. So only slightly more annoying than usual."

"He feels responsible."

"We all knew we had to go to that parlay, no matter how much it looked like a trap." He glanced at me. "Any problems reported from any of your settlements?"

I shook my head. "It looks like the vamps elsewhere were holding back waiting to see how last night played out. I doubt we'll get another reprieve tonight."

We might have left the room then, our combined uselessness heavy enough to push us into motion, but Serenity stirred. She rubbed at her face and shoved herself upright on the bed. Her gaze rested on Nate for a moment, her mouth twisting, and then rose to us.

"What's happening?"

"Nothing," I said quickly. "He's still healing, just... slowly. We have to assume he is, at least. He hasn't taken any turns for the worse."

She got up and walked to the side of the Nate's bed, resting her hand on the bear shifter's arm. "But he hasn't woken up at all?"

"It's pretty normal for us to need a good long sleep when we've been severely injured, princess," Marco put in. "To make sure we don't go running around straining those internal organs all over again while they're still piecing themselves back together."

"I don't know. That just sounds like a coma to me. And sometimes people don't come out of those."

"Shifters aren't your regular sort of person," Marco said archly. "And alpha shifters least of all." But the tilt of his head was a little stiff. Nate wasn't out of the woods yet.

Our dragon shifter could clearly tell that too. Her expression held so much worry that I had to go to her. Marco shot us a look and then drifted away.

"Hey," I said, tugging Serenity to me. "He's hanging in there. The fact that he's still with us after the wounds he took last night is a very good sign. We've got centuries of history behind us. Shifters are a tough bunch. It's not all going to end just because some vampires got some ridiculous notions into their heads."

My mate gave me a pained smile. Then she bobbed up on her toes to kiss me. I leaned into it, reveling in the softness of her lips and the sweet scent of her skin.

Wishing I could offer her more reassurance than I already had.

Ren

I finally peeled myself away from Nate's side when I realized it was past noon and I'd already lost half of the day. I didn't want to leave my mate, but the vampires were no doubt preparing for a full-out assault tonight. If there was anything I could do to protect the rest of my kin, I needed to be here to do it. They were counting on me.

Walking down the halls in a bit of a daze, little aches shooting through my legs where my wounds weren't quite healed, it took me a minute before the change in atmosphere registered. There was a bustling sort of energy moving through the estate. And more kin than I remembered seeing before. A lot more.

When I emerged from the halls into the central common rooms, unfamiliar figures were scattered all over, filling the chairs and sofas, clustered around the tables and doorways. A hum of nervous chatter and a cacophony of shifter scents surrounded me.

Not all of those scents were canine. A group of avian shifters had collected in one corner. A haggard but alive Leonard had been joined by several other feline shifters where he sprawled in an armchair at the other side of the room.

I spotted West coming in from the front yard as I

passed the main door. He was talking with Bertrand. I waited until he'd dismissed his lieutenant to go over.

"What's going on?" I asked, motioning to the crowded rooms.

He gave me a tight smile. "We're evacuating the shifter settlements closest to the main vampire hubs. As many as we can reasonably house on the estates. There'll be a lot of bed sharing and sleeping on the floor, but the fewer boundaries we have to defend, the better we can defend those that matter."

That made sense. And it made sense that the evacuated shifters would come to the estate closest to them, even if it wasn't the main center for their kin. I let out my breath. "And everything's ready around the estate? If we need more fire here?"

He nodded. "We've been ready since yesterday evening, but I had my people expand the barrier." His gaze slid down my body. I'd thrown on a simple shirt dress without much thought. The thin cotton only hung to my knees, exposing the scars below. The sting of last night's wounds prickled at me again.

"You should be resting, not walking around," West said. "You were hit pretty bad last night."

"*Nate* was hit bad," I said, with a sudden wrench of my heart. A fresh wave of anxiety passed through me, the image of his slumped body and slack face rising in the back of my mind. "Is there anything else your people can do to help him? They had Kylie up and walking around after she was torn up so bad before, and she's not even a shifter."

West's stance stiffened. "My kin have done

everything they can," he said sharply. "He'd be dead if they hadn't. I look after my people, and that includes everyone under the protection of my estate."

I blinked at him, thrown by the sudden change in his temper. "I didn't mean—"

West was already shaking his head. "It doesn't matter, Sparks. You just get on with whatever you feel you need to be doing."

He stalked off before I could say anything else, leaving me feeling strangely adrift. What had just happened there? Had we even been having the same conversation?

"Still not getting along so well with Mr. Wolf?" Kylie said, tucking her hand around my elbow as she came up beside me.

"Apparently," I said. "I'm not even sure what was bothering him this time."

"Well, it's not exactly the most relaxing of days, is it?" My best friend tipped her head against my shoulder. "I heard about Nate. And about how the whole vampire thing went down. Seems like I made a very wise decision sitting that one out. Is he going to be okay?"

"No one's sure yet," I said, swallowing hard. "He looks like he's healing. But it's not like anyone's made me any promises, so I guess that's not a guarantee." And how long could healing from that many bullets take? One of them had only barely missed his heart. What if he *couldn't* heal completely?

"He's a tough guy," Kylie said. She squeezed my arm. "I'm sure if he's made it this far, he'll pull through."

"That's what I want to think."

A slim figure with tawny hair emerged from the bustle—Felix. He was carrying a plate with a few sandwiches and some sliced veggies. "Dragon shifter," he said with a bob of his head. "I wanted to thank you for having our backs last night. Those bloodsuckers got what they deserved. And also, have you had anything to eat? I know you've been with the bear alpha since we got back."

He hesitated, looking suddenly uncertain. "He fought well for us, too. I'm sorry I couldn't take down the vamp that got to him first."

My chin wobbled, but I managed to smile. "Me too. Thank you. I can't say I'm hungry, but it'd probably be better if I got some food in me."

I accepted the plate, picking up one of the sandwiches and then offering the spread to Kylie. She raised an eyebrow at Felix. "Is this for the dragon shifter only, or is her human friend allowed to chow down too?"

He made a face, but the lowering of his eyes was embarrassed rather than annoyed. "I saw the supplies you were able to arrange to have brought in. Pretty impressive. I think you've earned at least a sandwich."

"Hmm," Kylie said, grinning. "I wonder what I'd have to do to earn a prime steak. Or a nice big slice of chocolate cake."

Felix's eyes widened. "I don't think we have any cake at the moment."

Kylie laughed. "I'm kidding. It's okay. Thank you for the sandwich. And no hard feelings. I'm used to being underestimated."

Felix looked a bit confused. Then he smiled back. "I'll make sure not to do it again."

Marco had slipped into the hall. Timothy, the lieutenant the vampires had roughed up before sending him to us with their message, was walking carefully but steadily beside him, nodding at something his alpha had said. This was the first time I'd seen him up and around since he'd staggered in here yesterday.

"Back to dragon shifter duty," I said to Kylie and Felix. I hurried over to the jaguar shifter and his companion.

"Princess," Marco said with a smile. He pressed a kiss to the side of my head. "My lieutenant was just telling me about what the dregs of the rogue group have been up to."

My eyebrows rose. I turned to Timothy. "Last night their king mentioned that the rogues had been talking with him. Did you see them?"

The lieutenant inclined his head. "Only a handful of them. From what I gathered, that's all that's left of the group they once had. At least, all who are still planning to keep fighting. But they know they don't stand a chance against you and our alphas. There was one grizzled old guy there—I didn't get close enough to scent him, but he looked canine. He seemed to be leading the stragglers. And he's led them right into the vampires' grasp."

I grimaced. "How can they ally with the vamps? Don't they know the king hates all shifters?"

Timothy shrugged. "They weren't acting very friendly with each other. The bloodsuckers were pushing them around some. But I guess to those few it mattered more to them to finish their fight than what happens to them after."

"Too much pride and not enough sense," Marco said, wrinkling his nose. "Well, they'll learn their final lesson pretty soon, I'd be willing to bet." He patted his lieutenant on the arm. "You did a good job, Timothy. Keep focusing on your recovery for now."

"Have you checked in on Nate again?" I asked my mate as Timothy ambled off.

Marco nodded. "No change. Is there anything I can do to help out here?"

"I don't know," I said. *I* still had to find some way to help prepare for whatever the vamps had in store for us tonight. But thinking about my last interaction with West, the prospect of asking him for ideas felt pretty daunting.

Marco must have read some of that feeling in my expression. He touched my cheek. "Is something else wrong?"

"No. I just—" I bit my lip. "West seemed angry with me. I'm not sure if I did something wrong somehow last night—I *did* lose control of my fire—or... I mean, it's not like it's strange for him to be grouchy, this just seemed a little more extreme than usual."

Marco gave me a crooked grin. "I don't think that's about you, princess. Wolf boy—well, let's just say I'm sure recent events are stirring up a lot of uncomfortable emotions for him. And he does seem to have difficulty processing those emotions without getting them all over everyone around him."

I frowned. "What do you mean?" Obviously the vampire attack had upset all of us, but Marco sounded like he was hinting at more than that.

The jaguar shifter shrugged. "It's not really my place to talk about it. He'd probably bite my head off—maybe literally. But I don't mind pointing you in the right direction. Next time you have the chance, get him to talk about his mother."

CHAPTER 7

Ren

THE LATE AFTERNOON sun had already dipped to the tops of the trees, but it still managed to blaze against my dark hair. "Is that the last of it?" I asked, wiping sweat from my forehead.

The canine shifters glanced along the line of hastily chopped firewood we'd already heaped up just outside the estate wall. "I think we've done all we can," Bertrand said. "We'd be able to keep this fire going for a good long time. If we even need to, with your dragon fire on our side." He shot me a respectful smile.

At least West's kin figured I could hold my own.

"I think it's just about time for dinner," Felix said, licking his lips. The faint smell of roasting meat was drifting over the estate wall from the house. My own stomach gurgled.

We tramped across the cleared earth around the ring

and through the gate. Bertrand shut the door with a thump and locked it. Then we all filed into the dining hall.

The canine estate wasn't quite as posh as some of the others, but the dining hall was still impressive. Huge oak beams crisscrossed the high ceiling all through the immense space. Heavy rugs overlapped each other under the matching oak tables, each of which was large enough to seat twenty. Light danced in sconces all along the walls, even though enough daylight streamed through the windows at the head of the room to make them unnecessary.

The roasting smell thickened as we stepped inside. My gaze snagged on the head table by those front windows, the one meant for me and my mates. Normally I'd have sat there with West by my side, for him to show me off the way the other alphas had. But since the estate was crowded with refugees, the tables were merely being used for serving now, with everyone eating on their feet as they circulated through the room.

I spotted Aaron and Marco at the far end of the space, but I couldn't see the canine alpha.

Would West even have wanted to show me off? We'd barely had a chance to really talk since we'd arrived. And I couldn't blame that on him, not really. The vampires had kept us plenty busy.

What did his kin make of the fact that he hadn't consummated our bond yet? They still seemed to treat me as if they considered me *their* dragon shifter.

All I knew was the uncertainty dragged at me—like a rough wind that washed over me every time I thought about that missing piece in my role as dragon shifter. In my *life*. I was meant to stand united with all four of the alphas, all four of my mates. And one of them continued to keep his distance. Another now lay on what could turn out to be his deathbed.

I was pretty sure this was not the future my mother had meant for me when she'd spent all that time trying to keep me safe. In fact, I'd be willing to bet this kind of danger and turmoil was exactly what she'd hoped to keep me out of.

At least my chances of surviving this situation were a lot better than they'd been when I was five. Small victories.

Bertrand moved to grab some pork tenderloin off one of the tables, and I made myself follow him. I couldn't afford to dwell on my worries right now. As far as I was concerned, every shifter in this room was my kin. They needed me girding myself for the battle ahead, not wallowing in whatever dire possibilities my imagination could come up with.

I chewed and smiled and chatted with the many canine kin—and a few avians—who came over to meet me. The canine shifters were as fawning as the ones I'd met before, but their eyes looked a little haunted. I found myself reassuring them again and again. "We won't let the vampires win. I'll see that they pay for what they've already done. The one thing they can't beat is dragon fire."

Even though I knew that wasn't entirely true. The vamps could shoot through the flames. And I couldn't promise I'd have enough, not when I hadn't shielded Nate quickly enough yesterday.

I'd eaten about as much as my stomach would take around the knots it'd tied itself in when I caught a glimpse of West near the doorway. He was just popping a last piece of flatbread into his mouth with a nod to the attendant he'd been talking to. Then he ducked out the door.

I didn't let myself think. I just hurried after him.

The wolf shifter was vanishing around the bend when I reached the hall. I jogged over in time to see him turning into another room just past the kitchens. What the heck was he doing over there?

When I reached that door, I paused before easing it open. On the other side, West's head jerked up.

He was standing in what appeared to be a storage room. Several metal tanks were stacked against one wall. They gave off a dull yellow shine in the dim light of the overhead bulb. A sour tang tickled my nose.

"Kerosene," West said, noticing my puzzled stare. "We keep a stock of it to hold us over in case there's a problem with the natural gas line. We're pretty isolated out here. In the winter... Anyway, I was thinking we might want to have them more readily at hand. In case we need extra fuel."

"Oh. That could be a good idea." I took a step inside, letting the door swing shut behind me. My skin twitched with an increased awareness of how small the room was. How little distance remained between me and my wolf shifter.

West rubbed his temple and ran his fingers back

through his hair, the silver strands glinting amid the light auburn. He looked at me, his mouth flat, his eyes unreadable.

"I'm sorry about how I talked to you earlier," he said in a tone brisk but not quite dismissive. "I've got too much on my mind. Too much to keep track of. Is there something you needed?"

It wasn't the most effusive apology I'd ever gotten, but I could see the strain in him so clearly that any hurt I'd held on to melted. "No," I said, and then reconsidered. When would we get another chance to talk like this? That was why I'd followed him, wasn't it?

I sucked in a breath. "Actually, there is. I just—I want to understand. This war, or whatever it is, with the vampires... It's weighing on you more than the other alphas."

West let out a hoarse chuckle. "We're on my territory here. This is my estate. The difference between host and guests, Sparks."

I fixed him with an insistent look. "It's more than that." Because he'd been more on edge, more worried about possible consequences of any conflict we faced, from before we'd had any idea the vampires might attack. From the moment he'd met me. And, hell, maybe even before, for all I could know about that. "Marco said I should ask you about your mother."

West muttered something under his breath that sounded like it contained several curse words and the word "cat." He shook his head, moving to brush past me to the door. "You don't want to hear that story."

I grabbed his arm, just above the elbow, with enough

strength to halt him. To remind him that he might be alpha, but he was talking to a dragon.

"Yes," I said. "I do."

West met my eyes straight on for the first time since I'd come into the room. I felt suddenly hot, standing that close to him, my bare hand against the solid curve of his bicep. But I held his gaze. I wasn't backing down, not this time.

"Fine," he said, stepping away from the door and from me in the same movement. Just like that, I could breathe again.

The wolf shifter turned his head as if inspecting the tanks. "There isn't much to it. There's a major fae habitation not far from here. We had a clash with them when I was fifteen. They'd told earlier alphas we could settle on a part of their territory they were no longer using themselves. Then they changed their minds. Some of the younger shifters mouthed off at the fae who barged in to tell us to leave. I tried to make peace, but I'd only been alpha for four years."

"And you were only fifteen," I said. My heart was already sinking with the sense of where this story was going.

"Old enough to know my responsibilities," West said. "They thought we were weak, that they had an excuse to root us out and grab some of our domain to add to theirs at the same time. They hit the village by the border of those grounds. We all went out to fight, all of us able-bodied."

He hesitated. When he spoke again, his voice was rigidly even. "The fae were coming at us from all over. I was alpha. I was giving the orders. My parents had come to fight too. My mother was practically beside me. One of the fae came at her out of nowhere, knocked her over with a blast.

"I could have jumped in. I might have saved her life. But at the same time a whole charge of fae rushed at us from the front lines, where most of the fighting was, and my kin there started to falter..."

He stopped. The silence hung for a long moment. "I raced to the front," he said. "As fast as I could. Called everyone to me. Took down three of the glowy bastards myself. If I hadn't, it would have been a slaughter. We'd have lost at least a dozen more lives. We might have lost the whole village. Instead we pushed them back."

A lump had filled my throat. "But your mother died."

"Yes," he said harshly. "That's what real loyalty is, Sparks. I swore to serve my kin as much as they serve me. I could have been selfish and put one person I cared about over the good of the pack, but then I'd have been a wretch of an alpha. I have to put them first, always. Every time they show their throats to me, they're telling me they know I don't take *their* loyalty lightly. I won't let them down."

"And everyone knows about the choice you made." Marco had known about it, and the canine and feline kin weren't exactly buddy-buddy.

West shrugged stiffly. "There was a lot of talk, at the time. Mostly because my father didn't agree with that choice. He saw what happened, but he was too far away to help my mother himself. He hasn't spoken to me since that battle."

I stared at him. When West was fifteen—his father had held that decision over him, a decision that had saved so many lives, for twelve *years*? "You were practically still a kid."

"I was alpha," West said, his gaze coming back to me as if daring me to blame him too.

But I didn't. I wouldn't have blamed him if he had saved his mom in that moment, but he'd made a sacrifice instead. One life to save several more, to protect a village, to turn the tide of the battle. I couldn't imagine it. If it'd been *my* mom—

The realization hit me then, like a smack in the face. It took me a few seconds to even form the words.

"You must have hated my mother," I said. "For what she did. For leaving all of you, for all that time. Just to protect me." By his standards, she'd been so terribly weak.

I didn't expect to see West's expression soften. "Ren..." he said. "I did. For a long time. But I don't know what it's like, being in those shoes. Having all the additional responsibilities that come with being dragon shifter. Maybe running and saving you was the best thing she could have done for us. It certainly could have gone a hell of a lot worse."

We could all have died, and the dragon shifter line could have died out completely. Was he saying he was sure now that his kin were better off with me than each kin-group fending for themselves?

"Anyway," West went on, "As a fellow alpha, Nate might as well be my kin too. If I'd gotten in there a little faster last night, before that vampire pulled the trigger..." He exhaled raggedly. "I carry *that* responsibility. All of us alphas need to stay strong. United. I'd hate to see what the bloodsuckers do to us if we fall apart."

And what about after the vampires were dealt with? Did he see us staying united then?

My pulse had sped up, thumping hard in my chest. "West," I said, "if you—"

A wordless shout of alarm rang down the hall. Both of us whirled toward the door.

"They're here!" someone called out. "The vampires are outside the walls."

CHAPTER 8

Ren

"Away from the doors!" West shouted as we dashed through the jostling crowd to the front doors. "If you've got an assigned task, join me outside. Everyone else, stay in the house. You're safest behind these walls. That's an order!"

I could taste the fear in the air, like an acrid chill. Uneasy murmurs traveled all around us. My heart thudded. Evacuating all these kin to this estate meant fewer walls to defend, but it also meant a whole lot more depended on us holding these particular walls. We couldn't let even one vampire break through.

I burst past the door with a bunch of West's guards and other kin who were joining the battle. Sandra, the wolf shifter he'd sent scouting this afternoon, fell into step beside us. Her face was flushed, her breath short. "I headed back as soon as I saw the trucks. I can't have gotten more than a few minutes lead on them. They'll be here any—"

The growl of engines sounded on the other side of the walls. And here they were. West swung his arm. "To your assigned positions. Everyone, ready. We'll take them down just like we discussed."

I knew my role in all of this. I wanted to say something to West, to show how much I appreciated him opening up to me, but our enemies were right outside. I couldn't waste a second.

And after the story he'd just told me, I knew he wouldn't want me to anyway.

I yanked off my dress as I hurried down the front steps and launched myself into the air. My wings snapped from my frame, expanding as the rest of my body did too. No relaxed shift this time. My muscles screamed and my nerves twanged. But I was up in the sky, scaled and soaring, before the first vampires had even emerged.

Truck doors slammed. Feet crunched into the brush. Guns clicked, ready to fire. Was the king himself out there?

After the way he'd ducked out of the battle last night, I doubted it. Here was West leading our defense on the front lines, and the leader of our enemies couldn't even be bothered to show up to watch the results of his orders.

I gritted my teeth, my dragon fangs rasping against each other. If I ever saw the vampire king again, I wasn't giving him the chance to barter for his life. He'd be a crispy cinder before he'd so much as blinked.

The bloodsuckers moved through the forest along the edge of the ring we'd cleared. Their pale forms blended in and out of the shadows. They were spreading out, circling the estate, as we'd expected. And not venturing too close to the cleared area with its heaped line of firewood. I guessed the purpose of that defense was pretty obvious.

But we didn't want to light it until we needed to. That wood would have to last us the whole night, until the sun drove any remaining vampires away.

West's people spread out too, taking their positions along the walls. Ready to leap over and light the fire if they needed to—or to fend off any vampires who tried to scale those walls. As I swooped over the front yard, Kylie emerged from one of the equipment sheds carrying the flame-thrower she'd had one of her contacts fashion. Felix's head jerked around in a double-take when she passed him. Oh yeah, he definitely wasn't underestimating her now.

But I didn't want any of my companions to have to leave the protection of these walls. If I could turn all the vamps to cinders before they breached the estate—and before my shift started to falter—there'd be no more kin joining Nate in the healer room tonight.

Gunfire rattled by the far end of the estate. I swung around to pinpoint the sound, and the vampires near the gate moved forward. Oh no, they weren't getting away with that. I banked sharply to the left, gathering flames in my throat.

My blast crackled over three of the bloodsuckers. Shots boomed from deeper between the trees. Bullets tore through the lower edge of my wings with a sharp stinging.

I swept upward, out of the guns' range, and then dove back down. One undead figure, and another, and another, was visible here and there between the trees. I caught two of them before they wrenched their guns up. The third opened fire.

I managed to yank myself to the side just in time to avoid the worst of the onslaught of bullets. A fresh stinging radiated through my right wing.

Below me, farther down the wall, a group of vamps had made a run at the estate. They leapt at the wall, flinging themselves higher than any living human could have jumped, heaving their guns with them to get in some early shots.

I careened toward them, withheld fire searing the back of my mouth. The shifter guard on the platform inside the wall bashed one of the intruder's skulls against the stone blocks. Kylie scrambled up to join him and took out another vamp with a spurt of her flame-thrower. They both ducked back down as guns crackled from the edge of the forest.

Then I was on the vamps. I breathed a scorching line of fire over the rest of the group clambering over the wall and whipped myself around to blast the ones hiding in the trees.

I couldn't tell how many I caught amid the blackened tree trunks. They were keeping too far back, just close enough to have a clear line of fire with their guns. The forest was too dense for me to pick them off easily, not without setting it all up in flames.

More gunfire rang out from the far end of the estate. I wheeled, flapping my wings harder. Even here, I couldn't be everywhere at once. But I had to take out more of the bloodsuckers before I pulled back and let that protective ring do the fiery work for me. There were too many still out there. If our ring burned out before dawn, if even a few vamps got past the walls, this battle would turn into a bloodbath.

I rained fire down on another group of vampires that had run at the wall. Two of the shifters were grappling with one who'd managed to scramble over. I swooped toward him. He got a couple shots off before the guards wrenched the gun away from him. Blood bloomed on one of the guard's shoulders. He slashed the vampire's throat.

As the undead body slumped into stasis, the guards jumped back, looking to me. Oh, I could finish the job, all right. I breathed a spear of flames down at the vampire, my lips curling into a dragonish smile as he burst into ashes.

My smile didn't last long. I wheeled back toward the forest, and a cacophony of shots split the air. All of them aimed at me. The vampires knew who the biggest threat to them was. I spewed flames across the edge of the forest, not quite quickly enough. The hail of bullets had been aimed at my wings again, where the scales were softest and the flesh thinnest.

I flapped my wings, pushing myself higher. The air coursed through the dappling of wounds, sparking pain with every movement. More shots echoed up from beneath me. More bullets tore through the tender flesh. I poured down more fire, but the guns kept booming. Each bullet bit through my body with a sharp throbbing. My thoughts started to splinter.

I had to keep going. Had to stop all of them. But there were too many, and my wings could barely hold me up now. Every brush of air against them was agony.

My focus narrowed through the haze of pain. I couldn't fall outside the walls. My kin would come to try to rescue me, and the vampires would slaughter them. But I could give my shifters one last gesture of protection. If I set our ring on fire, none of them would have to venture beyond the walls for that purpose either.

My wings wavered. Another hail of bullets sprayed over me, some tearing more holes in my wings, some glancing off my thicker scales, a few digging into my side. I sputtered up one last gush of flames aimed at the circle of chopped wood.

The logs and branches hissed. Flames leapt up all along the ring in a rippling dance. With a relieved smile, I hurled my plummeting body toward the wall.

My knee glanced off the stones, but I tumbled over the side into the estate. Voices were hollering and footsteps pounding toward me before I even hit the ground, already human again.

The impact sent a fresh wave of agony through my shoulders and down my back. I cried out, flinching against ground now slick with my blood. Then the pain hazed my mind completely, and the world went black.

My body came back into awareness gradually. First the

dull prickling of pain running all down my back and sides, where my dragon wings had crumpled back into my human form. A deeper ache searing through my ribs when I tried to roll over. A soft sheet was draped over me. Warring smells of blood and a sweet, clean perfume drifting through the air to my nose.

I managed to blink my eyes open.

"Ren!" Kylie said. She was standing over me at the edge of the bed, her hands fisted where they rested on the mattress. The pink tufts of her pixie cut were drooping and dark smudges underlined her eyes, but she gave me her most brilliant smile. "How do you feel? Should I call the healers?"

Of course. I was back here in the healer room again. Holding my body still, I took in my surroundings. Pale light was shining through the windows. Good, that meant we'd gotten to the morning without losing the estate. More forms were slumped under sheets around the room, but the rasps of sleeping breaths carried to my ears. They were all alive still.

Everyone in here, at least.

"Sore, but okay other than that," I said, meeting Kylie's gaze again. "I don't think I need any help. What happened last night? Is everyone else okay?"

"We held the vamps off," she said. "Some of the shifters were injured, but all of us survived."

That should have been amazing news, but her smile had faltered. I pushed myself into a sitting position, wincing as I went. My back throbbed, but I needed to know. "What's wrong? Something's bothering you."

"You are way too good at picking those things up," my

best friend said, waggling a finger at me. "And you should really stay lying down until someone checks you out again, I think."

When I didn't budge, Kylie let out a huff of breath. "I don't know what's wrong. But the vamps pulled back after the fire had been going a couple hours. They took off and didn't come back, but they didn't send any message about giving up the fight or anything. Your guys figure they're making some new plan now that they've seen our strategy."

Of course they were. I suppressed a groan. "Great. Well, I guess we can be glad we've got all day to prepare for whatever it is."

"And for you to recover," Kylie said, giving me a gentle shove. "You were really beat up, Ren. Just because you're a dragon doesn't mean you're immortal, you know."

"Believe me, I've never been more aware of that than right now." I stretched one arm and then the other, bracing myself against the twanging aches that shot through my muscles.

"I should go tell the guys. They'll want to know you're awake. They were hanging around looking worried for a really long while, you know, but then they had to get on with whatever alpha business needs taking care of. Maybe you'll listen to them about getting your rest even if you won't listen to me."

She wrinkled her nose at me, and I cracked a smile. Then a low rumble of a voice reached my ears from the bed behind me.

"You don't have to go far to tell me."

"Nate!" I threw myself around on the bed, so fast the pain sliced right through me. But seeing those warm brown eyes gazing back at me was worth the extra helping of agony. I scrambled right off the mattress and clambered onto his cot, slowing as I eased myself down beside him. If my body was aching this much after last night's wounds, I couldn't imagine how he must be feeling after the beating he'd taken.

My mate wrapped his brawny arm around my waist and tugged me even closer to him. I cuddled up to him, breathing in his musky, peppery scent. My heart swelled with joy. "I was so worried about you. You've been out a whole *day*, you know."

Nate let out a hoarse chuckle. "Looks like I should have been worried about you too. Throwing yourself into the middle of the battle like usual?"

"Someone's got to bring the firepower," I said. "Anyway, after that fight in the gas station, I don't think you're anyone to talk."

"Hmm. I'm definitely not looking to repeat that experience."

Kylie made an amused sound. "Well, I guess it doesn't matter which bed you're lying in as long as you're lying down. Don't get too frisky, is all I'm saying. I'll see if I can track down the other guys."

"Thank you," I called after her. I tipped my head back to kiss Nate and looped my arm around his back. The faint dimpling of his wounds made me hesitate. "I'm not hurting you, am I?"

"Ren," Nate murmured, "there is absolutely nowhere

I want you to be except right here. So don't you dare budge an inch."

He pressed a kiss to my forehead and adjusted his body so we fit together even more perfectly. I nestled in his warmth, letting my eyelids slide shut. We both deserved a little reprieve before we had to face whatever the vampires were going to throw at us next, didn't we?

CHAPTER 9

West

I STUDIED my scar in the mirror as I readied a fresh bandage. This morning, the pulse of the old wound was still threaded with angry red, but mostly its glow shone yellow. A sickly yellow like the twist of anxiety that wound through my chest.

I scowled at the patch of color before I pressed the bandage over it. Damned fae. Trust them to come up with a kind of injury that'd haunt you more than a decade later.

Granted, at the moment I was feeling even less pleased with the vampires. My scowl deepened as I shrugged on a clean shirt to replace the one I'd been too busy to change since sometime yesterday. I had my kin running around doing everything I could think of to be ready for tonight... but who the hell knew what tonight was going to bring? The bloodsuckers clearly weren't going to be happy until they'd slaughtered the lot of us.

Like they'd almost slaughtered Ren last night.

My pulse hitched at the memory of her falling, bullet-riddled body. I clenched my jaw and turned toward the door.

Just as the woman in question burst past it into my rooms.

My dragon shifter's eyes were bright with excitement, her face split with a beaming smile. But I could tell from her slight hesitation as she nudged the door shut behind her that she was still in some pain. She had to be. The last time I'd seen her, she'd been slumped unconscious on that healer room bed while her flesh knit itself back together.

"Nate's awake!" she said. "He's okay. Still a little weak from all the wounds, but okay."

Her scent reached me then, that fiery sweetness mixed with the bear shifter's musk. Because of course they'd been all over each other the second he'd come to.

A twinge of jealousy I knew was ridiculous shivered through me. She *should* have gone right to him. He was her mate, and he'd almost died. I clamped down on the twinge and shoved it aside, along with the half a dozen other emotions I was trying not to feel.

"And you should be back there in the healer room too, not running around to tell me," I said. "You're not fully recovered yet either."

"I *walked*," Ren said. "And I thought you'd want to know, after everything you said yesterday. Kylie found

Marco and Aaron, but you must have been off hiding somewhere."

"I just got back from making additional preparations farther down the highway," I said shortly. "I'd have found out soon enough. You should be more concerned about looking after yourself."

Was that a wince she'd stifled as she set her hands on her hips? For fuck's sake, she shouldn't be walking, or standing, or anything other than lying down right now.

"I'm fine," she said, in her usual stubborn way. "It was a tough fight, but we all got through it. You don't have to treat me like a weakling."

Did she not realize how close *she'd* come to dying? My temper escaped me. "I wouldn't if you'd finally learn you can't do everything. You practically got yourself killed out there, but we did still need that back-up fire last night, didn't we?"

Ren definitely flinched then. But not because of any injury. Because of my retort.

In a flash, I saw how her face had fallen, the joyful light gone out of her eyes. She'd come in here brimming with happiness she'd had every reason to feel, and I'd managed to crush it in less than a minute. My heart wrenched.

"I don't know..." Ren's voice wavered. She waved her arm vaguely, blinking as if trying to hold back tears. "I don't know what I'm doing wrong. But if after all this time you still don't think I'm enough, why don't you just tell the rest of us to leave so you can do whatever it is you think you're going to do without a dragon shifter?"

Her words tore through me. Did she really believe—

She was already spinning around, shoulders tensed, swiping at her eyes. I couldn't let her leave like that. Fuck plans, fuck principles, fuck good intentions. If this was where they'd gotten me, they obviously weren't worth much.

"Ren." I caught her elbow as she stepped toward the door. She turned back, her expression wary.

Suddenly I didn't know what to do with myself. I'd led hundreds of kin since I was a kid. Why was talking to this one woman so damned hard? She was meant for me.

And I was meant for her.

I rested my other hand against the wall beside her, leaning just close enough that I could feel the warmth emanating from her body. Not so close that she couldn't break my grasp and move away if that's what she wanted.

But she stayed there, gazing back at me. I swallowed thickly.

"I'm sorry," I said, forcing myself to keep looking back at her. If seeing the pain on her face hurt me too, well, that was my own damn fault. "You're more than enough. You're fucking spectacular, Ren. I'm sorry I ever made you feel otherwise. I don't know if *I'm* ever going to be worthy of *you*. But I'm going to try. I promise you that."

"West..." Her expression had turned puzzled. "But you— I thought— You've been acting like you're still not sure."

"That's not what I was aiming for. There just hasn't been a good time..." I didn't even know how to explain it. "I'm sure. I've been sure."

She blinked. "Since when?"

That one thing I could tell her. I could pinpoint the

exact moment my heart had flipped over and I'd realized what an idiot I'd been. I could still see her in that instant in my memory, naked and blood-streaked at the edge of the clearing, her eyes shining with grief.

"When we ambushed the rogues with the disparate kin. The way you tried to save that guard of Nate's. How upset you were when you couldn't. If you could care that much about a muskrat shifter who'd considered betraying us... I couldn't ask anything more for all our kin than compassion like that."

"That was—that was *days* ago, West. Why the hell haven't you said anything?"

I opened my mouth and closed it again, trying to find the words. My reasoning had all made a lot more sense when I'd only had to work it out in my own head.

"There was so much going on," I said. "The rogues and Marco's challenge and now the bloodsuckers wreaking havoc... I know I have a lot to make up to you, for how I treated you before. I didn't want to put any pressure on you to forgive me while you were dealing with everything else. When things have calmed down, when you have room to breathe—you can take your time deciding whether you can be sure of me. I can prove to you that I'll be a good mate. I—"

"Oh, West," Ren interrupted, so softly my pulse stuttered. She rested her hand against my chest. "You don't need to prove anything. I already know who you are. I want you. Now, if I can have you."

Now. That sounded like a very, very good idea. I stared at her, and all I could see in her eyes now was the same longing coursing through me.

She wanted me. She wanted *me*, even now, in spite of everything.

The dam cracked open inside me, releasing a surge of desire more powerful than I'd even known I was bottling up. I bridged the last short inches between us and captured Ren's mouth with mine.

My dragon shifter kissed me back just as hard. Her fingers curled into my shirt, tugging my body to hers, as her other hand rose to tease into my hair. I pressed her up against the wall, with just enough self-control to be careful of her injuries. She tasted and felt like heaven. Why had I denied myself this bliss for so goddamned long?

It didn't matter. I had her now. Had her arching against me as I gripped her thigh, had her whimpering at the sweep of my tongue over hers. The possessive impulse I'd tried to bury earlier rose up, and I didn't have the will left to rein it in.

I jerked her hips tight against mine, tipping her head so I could claim her mouth even more deeply. Her hands clasped behind my neck. She hummed eagerly, with a gasp as I released her lips to trail my tongue and teeth along her jaw.

"Mine," I muttered. "Mine." I hadn't really believed it until this moment. I wasn't sure I totally believed it even now.

"Yours," Ren agreed with a happy sigh. "And you're mine."

Something about those three simple words made my throat close up. I pulled back just enough to meet her eyes.

"I am. I've been yours since the first second I saw you, even if I was too bullheaded to accept it."

"Wolf-headed," she murmured with a breathless giggle, and I was lost again. I fell back into her, the heat of her mouth, the rocking of her body against mine, setting all of me on fire in a way I was all too happy to burn. My hand rose to cup her breast. I was stroking its peak harder through the thin cotton of her dress, marking my territory down the other side of her jaw with the graze of my teeth, when she lifted her chin.

In that first instant, I didn't catch the meaning of the gesture. Then she raised her head even higher, not just giving easier access but blatantly offering the entire pale expanse of her throat.

My breath stopped. For a second, all I could do was ogle the vulnerable skin she'd displayed for me so easily. The highest show of trust any of my kin could give another. An act of total submission, placing her life at my discretion.

How had I become worthy of an honor that great?

I'd better *be* worthy of it. I dipped my head, pressing the most tender kiss I had in me to the center of my mate's throat. I couldn't bring myself to do more than that.

"Oh, Sparks," I said, my voice hoarse. "You should never have to submit yourself to me."

Ren lowered her head to meet my eyes. The corner of her mouth quirked up. "I figured we could take turns. Keep things fair."

A rough chuckle broke from my mouth, and all I

could do was kiss her again. Firmly, hungrily, with all the passion I'd spent the last few weeks denying.

Ren

My lips slid against West's, and I reveled in the heat radiating off him. My nerves were already trembling with the bliss of having him here, like this, giving himself and taking me without restraint. But who was I kidding? I wanted more, so much more. I wanted everything.

My hands trailed down his chest to grip the hem of his shirt. I tugged it upward. With a hungry growl, West broke the kiss to tug the shirt off, capturing my mouth again an instant later. His fingers teased over my body until they found the zipper beneath my arm. One sharp yank, and the soft fabric of my dress was falling off me.

I hadn't bothered with a bra in my hasty departure from the healer room. My nipples pebbled as they grazed my mate's bare chest. I let out a whimper, kissing him harder, but a prickle of discomfort crept through the haze of pleasure. I *wasn't* completely healed, and my muscles were starting to protest about staying upright so long.

Well, I had no particular interest in staying upright any longer. I pushed West backward, toward the bed, careful of the bandage that covered his scar. He glanced behind him, and his lips curved into an eager grin. With a flash of his dark green eyes, he swept me off my feet. In a few swift strides, he'd thrown both of us onto the bed, him bending over me. Then his lips were pressed against mine again.

"Sparks," he murmured as he stroked my breasts. The nickname didn't sound like anything less than a reverent compliment now. His thumbs flicked over my nipples, and I moaned. My hips canted toward his of their own accord, wanting to feel him pressed against me there too. His hardness against my core.

He flipped us over in an easy motion, leaving me gazing down at him. Rising up on one elbow, he wove his fingers into my hair and claimed another kiss. I rocked against him, unable to help myself. The feel of that bulge beneath his jeans made me giddy.

West groaned. He eased back for a second, holding my gaze. Then, very deliberately, he tipped back his head to expose his whole throat to me.

My heart skipped a beat, or maybe two. I'd be willing to bet this man—this *alpha*—had never offered his throat to anyone except the alpha who'd come before him, years and years ago. I'd already believed everything he'd said when he'd told me how he felt, but seeing him volunteer that vulnerability to me made the truth of it hit me even harder.

I was his. And he was mine. All mine.

A little choked up, I eased down to kiss a gentle path from his jaw down the hollow of his throat, past his Adam's apple. Then I kept going. Down across the planes of chest, over his solid abs, to the buckle of his jeans. I could make short work of those. My knuckles brushed his erection as I tugged the zipper down. West sucked in a breath.

Before I could make good on my intentions, he grasped my shoulders and pulled me up the bed, rolling back on top of me in the same motion. His voice came out even more throaty than usual.

"If I'm going to be inside any part of you, there's only one place I want to be."

A flood of heat washed through my sex, as if he were already there. "So get on with it already," I said. "Do you have any idea how long I've been waiting to properly call you my mate?"

West made a rough sound. Then his mouth crashed down on mine as if he were desperate to taste me again. We wrenched his jeans off together, and somewhere in there my panties disappeared. His hands teased over my thighs as the hard length of his cock rubbed against my clit. I whimpered, clutching at him and raising my legs by his waist to urge him on.

A tremor ran through West's entire body. Then he was plunging into me, all the way to the hilt in one thrust. A moan burst from my lips.

"Ren," West murmured in time with his strokes. "Ren." Like he was laying claim and saying a prayer at the same time. The glow of our bond radiated through me, so bright my vision hazed. Bright and completely solid for the first time, as that rush of warmth joined the rest of the ties to my four alphas inside my chest.

I had my mates, all of them, exactly as it was meant to be.

West drove into me, filling me, completing me with that giddy burn. I caressed my hands over every inch of his skin that I could reach, the muscles coiling in his shoulders and down his chest. I bucked to meet his strokes. My breath broke into pants. With each pump of his hips he sent me higher, a wave of pleasure building and building until I was trembling with it.

He arched, bending to slick his tongue over one of my nipples. His cock surged inside me at a tighter angle, and my orgasm crackled through me like a firework. I gasped, clenching around him. His breath hitched too. "Fuck," he muttered, bucking harder. His muscles twitched beneath my gripping fingers. With a groan, he followed me into release.

We rocked to a stop, our skin damp with sweat where our bodies pressed together. A pleased sounding hum reverberated from my mate's chest. He lowered himself beside me, tucking his arm around my waist, his nose brushing my cheek.

"Mine," he murmured one last time.

I smiled and squirmed over to hug him back. "Mine."

CHAPTER 10

Ren

I DOZED FOR A FEW MINUTES, until a strange light hazing my eyelids brought me back to sharper awareness. I blinked, nuzzling closer to West and breathing the smell of his skin, like rich earth and the pines outside.

Somewhere in the midst of our coming together, his bandage had fallen off. The glow I'd noticed was emanating from his scar. I'd never seen it this close before: a slight indent in his skin with ragged edges marking the boundaries of a magical blast.

I raised my fingers to it tentatively. The surface of the scar was smooth, harder than the rest of his skin but just as warm. When West didn't pull away, I lay my palm right against it.

"It changed color," I said.

"It does that," West said. "What were you expecting?"

"I think it's always been red when I've seen it before." Now it was beaming a vibrant pink. Not a color I'd have expected West to sport, but I guessed he didn't have a whole lot of choice in the matter.

"That would make sense. You've probably only seen it when I was throwing myself into some kind of skirmish. Angry."

It took a moment for that information to sink in. I looked up at him. "It shows your emotions?"

He shrugged. I could tell from the slight tensing of his shoulders that he didn't enjoy discussing this topic, but he held my gaze anyway. "Fae magic works in strange ways."

"No wonder you keep it covered up." Imagine going around alpha-ing with all your kin being able to read anything you were feeling from the glow through your shirt. Wearing your heart on your sleeve pretty much literally. "You got it during that fight when your..."

"When they killed my mother," he filled in when I faltered. "Yes. It was red for a pretty long time after that."

I ran my thumb along the edge where the scar met the softer skin over his leanly muscled chest. "So what does pink mean?"

West chuckled. "Do you really need to ask that, Sparks?"

He tipped my chin up to bring my mouth to his. The kiss was so long and tender it left me feeling as if my heart were glowing too. Our lips parted, our faces still close enough to brush noses.

"I love you, Ren," he said, low and rough.

My pulse skipped. I looped my arm around his neck, tugging all of me closer to him. "I love you too."

"Lord only knows how I got that lucky."

I laughed. "You didn't exactly make it easy when we got started." But there were some things I didn't totally understand about how he'd reacted to me. "You were worried I was going to take off on your kin—all the kin— when the going got tough, like my mother did?"

He shrugged. "That was some of the problem. I wanted to be sure we could count on you before I put their lives in your hands. And also, especially later on... I wanted you. I didn't know how much to trust my judgment. I have to put what my kin need over what I want, so when my instincts seem to be telling me what they need just happens to be something I'd very much enjoy, I have trouble not being skeptical."

"Maybe you're a little too hard on yourself," I suggested.

"Maybe." He exhaled a ragged breath. "Ever since that battle, and losing my mother— It might not make total sense, but I've always had this feeling hanging over me that if I make a selfish choice for something else, I'm saying she didn't matter enough. If I was willing to sacrifice her and not something else."

My throat tightened. I nuzzled his cheek. "You're definitely too hard on yourself. I guess I can forgive you for being hard on me too."

He gave a hoarse guffaw. "You have no idea how much it's been killing me watching you throw yourself into harm's way, again and again..."

"That's my job," I said. "Just like it's yours."

"I know. That's why I don't stop you."

"You just mutter about it like a jerk."

"Hey." He bumped his nose against mine. "You *have* been known to place heroics a little too far over your own safety from time to time."

I smiled. "Hmm. Well, if we're comparing irrational behavior, where do we put 'making up for being a jerk by acting like an even bigger jerk' on that scale?"

"I'm not sure if 'bigger jerk' is a fair assessment. I was trying to ease off on you."

"Funny how easing off included an awful lot of snarking. And, you know, there was always the option of saying how you actually felt."

"Before or after you were done getting yourself almost killed, *again*?"

"Either would have been fine." I poked him in the sternum, peering up at him through my eyelashes. "Of course, given your usual fluency at sharing feelings, I might have ended up thinking you were telling me to jump off a cliff instead."

West caught my hand. With a growl, he rolled on top of me, pinning both my wrists above my head. "I think I can make my intentions a little more clear than that," he said, the gleam in his eyes both amused and heated.

I squirmed beneath him, the playful hold getting me all kinds of heated up too. My breath caught at the hardness I felt pressed against my thigh. In an instant, I was twice as wet. "Already up and at 'em again?" I said, wriggling a little more to the side so his cock could settle against my core.

The contact made us both groan. West grinned down at me. "I do have a few impressive qualities."

"Mmhm?" An ache of need was already spreading up from low in my belly. "Then by all means, go ahead and make full use of them."

The heat in his eyes turned blazing. "Oh, believe me, I will."

He bent to kiss me as he slid back inside me, and we gave ourselves over to pleasure for just a little while longer.

After a quick detour back to my rooms to find a dress that didn't look as if it'd recently been torn off in the throes of passion, I headed back through the mansion's halls to see where I was needed. I couldn't keep drifting along in the bliss of having finally consummated all of my mate-bonds for the rest of the day. The vampire threat hadn't gone away just because West and I had gotten it on.

West's kin and the others who'd taken shelter here were already hard at work laying down more firewood in the protective ring. Others had ventured farther away to scout out where the vampires might be holing up during the day. If they'd found temporary shelter somewhere, maybe we could turn the tables on them before night fell again.

If only it would be that easy. Somehow I doubted the bloodsuckers would have suddenly turned that careless.

I was just veering toward the common areas when the outline of a closed door snagged my attention from the corner of my eye. A jolt of anticipation I couldn't explain shot through me. I turned

The hall around me faded away.

I was standing in front of a simple door, this one painted the same pale moss green as the walls on either side of it. A circle of dimples marked its surface just above my eye level. It had no knob, no handle. A faint ringing filled my ears, and the certainty rose up in my mind that I could open that door if I wanted to. That it was meant for me to open—for me and my kind.

A familiar smell, like sweet clover and sunbaked stone, wrapped around me. *Home.* Then the vision washed away.

I stumbled backward, my still-sore back hitting the opposite wall.

The door I was looking at now, here in the canine estate, was light yellow-gold. It had a perfectly ordinary knob where a knob should be. But it had stirred something up in my memory—or maybe not my memory, but something deeper, that ran down through my dragon-shifter spirit. Excitement jittered through my nerves.

I'd come fully into my role. I was bonded with all four of my alphas, and through them with their kin. Maybe there'd been a lot more that came with being a dragon waiting for me than I'd ever even realized.

Maybe enough to stop the vampires attacks for good.

I spun away from the door and hurried the rest of the way into the common rooms. My gaze halted on the first attendant I saw. I caught her arm. "Can you find all the alphas and ask them to meet in our lounge? I need to see them immediately."

She bobbed her head. "Right away, dragon shifter."

I knew Nate was already in the lounge area that was just for me and my alphas to share. He'd left his healer room cot so he could make some calls to his kin without disturbing the other injured shifters.

When I burst into the room, he looked up from the armchair where he was sitting. His eyebrows rose. "Is everything okay, Ren?"

"I think so," I said. "I think I might know where we can find some answers. Are you well enough to travel?"

Nate pushed himself slowly but steadily to his feet. "I am if that's what we need to do. What happened?"

"I'm... not completely sure yet."

Marco sauntered into the room, his stance casual but his indigo eyes sharply alert. West stalked in a moment later with Aaron close behind him.

As they all came to a halt around me, a tremor passed through the air. It quivered over my skin, stealing my breath just for a second. This was the first time my alphas and I had all been in the same space with our bonds confirmed. The power of it hummed between us, almost electric.

I obviously wasn't the only one who could feel it. Marco smirked and cut his gaze toward West. "I take it you finally figured out how to remove your head from your ass."

The wolf shifter bared his teeth a sliver, but he couldn't seem to help smiling when his eyes rested on me. So this was what it really felt like, being the dragon shifter. Being the hub that held the shifter community together. The sensation was exhilarating and a little frightening at the same time.

"What's going on, Serenity?" Aaron asked.

I groped after the impression that had made me call for them. "The dragon shifter estate. You've been there at some point, haven't you? What color are the walls inside?"

My mates looked puzzled. "From what I can remember, they're green," Nate said. "Most of them, anyway. Why?"

"This feeling came over me just a few minutes ago," I said. "Like the visions my mother left for me—or the one I had of how she died. I saw a door in what I think was the dragon shifter's estate. It felt like home. And the color matches."

"A door," West repeated, giving me space to go on.

"I got the impression I'm meant to open it. Now that... Now that I'm completely bonded with all of you. That there's something on the other side I need, something intended for every dragon shifter. What if it's something that could help us against the vampires?"

The guys exchanged a glance. "That estate does hold secrets only the dragon shifters have ever understood," Aaron said. "When I visited with the alpha who mentored me, there was a whole section of the house we weren't allowed into. The records we have of the dragon shifter line have always been tenuous."

"What are you suggesting, princess?" Marco said. "Time for a field trip?"

I nodded. "I have to go, to find out what's there. The rest of you..."

"We're coming," West said firmly. "My lieutenants can keep our preparations going here, and lead our defenses if need be. Leaving you unguarded could be exactly what the vampires are waiting for. There's a jet here. We can be at your estate by the early afternoon."

That was all I'd needed to hear. I let out my breath. "Then let's get on that plane."

CHAPTER 11

Ren

Kylie draped herself across her seat on the private jet with a pleased sigh. "I could totally get used to this kind of luxury. Forget flying coach ever again."

I laughed. "I think most of the time we'll drive places. But the shifter cars I've been in have been pretty nice too. The jets are for emergencies."

"Very, very comfortable emergencies," my best friend declared, snuggling deeper into the smooth leather. "I've got no idea what those vampires could have been complaining about. Shifters know how to live right."

There'd been no way I was leaving Kylie behind again, not with another vampire attack on the horizon. And it wasn't as if she'd have let me anyway. I'd barely managed to tell her I'd decided I needed to visit the dragon shifter estate before she'd been grabbing the suitcase she'd brought from New York and announcing she was ready to go.

I thought she might even have convinced the attendants to haul that flame-thrower of hers into the cargo hold. But Aaron had looked over everything, and if he didn't think it was likely to blow us up, I guessed I shouldn't worry.

"There are some benefits to being in with the shifters, huh?" Felix said with a light grin. West had brought a few of his kin along for the ride to help set my former home in order after all those years of disuse. The fennec fox had settled himself into one of the seats across from us. At first I'd assumed his choice was a coincidence, but seeing the way his eyes gleamed watching Kylie, I wasn't so sure anymore.

"Oh, I can think of lots of reasons to stick around," Kylie said, grinning back. She ticked off her fingers. "Lots of feasts. Super comfy guest rooms. The company of my best friend, of course. And let's not forget all the amazing eye candy."

Had my bestie just… fluttered her eyelashes a little at Felix? And was he *blushing*? A hint of red had definitely colored the fox shifter's cheeks. He swept back his tawny hair, playing casual. "Sounds like you're exactly where you need to be, then."

"Oh, I'm sure of that."

"We have a lot more fun when there aren't vamps trying to massacre us. You should come back to the estate after we've crushed them."

"And you'll show me a good time?" Kylie said, her

grin widening. Oh, she was absolutely flirting with him. I'd know that *come get me* smile anywhere.

"Felix, come here a second," West called from closer to the front of the plane. The fox shifter made an apologetic grimace and hustled to see what his alpha wanted. I followed his path automatically, my gaze rising to meet West's. My mate's expression had been serious, but his eyes softened just a bit as he gave me a quick smile. And fuck if that wasn't enough to make my heart flutter.

"Hmm," Kylie said, waggling her eyebrows. "Is it just me, or is there more of a glow around you today? Any secrets you're ready to share?"

Now *I* was blushing. I ducked my head as heat washed over my face. But I couldn't stop a grin of my own from splitting my face.

An awful lot of things in our lives sucked right now— uh, some of them literally. But there wasn't a bloodsucker in the world that could take away the joy of having all my mates around me. Knowing we were all here for each other.

"Later," I said. "When we've got a little more privacy to chat." No doubt West's kin had already sensed the shift in atmosphere. It was kind of hard to tell if they were being more effusive toward me now when they'd been incredibly fawning from the start. But I'd caught a new sparkle in several eyes as we'd made our way through the mansion on our way out.

I was going to guess there'd be a whole lot of new canine kids running around about nine months from now, vampires or no. That didn't mean I wanted to be talking about my encounter with West where any of them could hear me with those sharp shifter ears.

"Oooh. I knew it!" Kylie said. "You're on fire, Ren. I mean, in a totally metaphorical, not at all dangerous sort of way."

The flutter came back into my chest, like a flickering of flames. "It does kind of feel like that," I had to admit.

"It's about time. No more being jerked around. Just love, love, love."

She said it in such a goofy singsong voice that I had to laugh again. That was why I loved *her*. For a few minutes, talking with her, I could forget all the other crap we still had to deal with.

At least, until Marco sank into the seat Felix had vacated, tucking his phone into his pocket. His mouth was set in his usual crooked smile, but his eyes were shadowed. Nate turned where he was sitting one seat over to see what the jaguar shifter had to say.

"A few of my people followed the vamps that came at my estate last night," he said. He'd been talking to one of his lieutenants in Florida. "It appears they've holed up in a smaller city that's closer to our territory than their usual haunt. Faster access for their next attack."

"Can your kin take the attack to them?" I asked. "Use daylight to our advantage?"

Marco shook his head. "The building they've taken over is too secure. Every nook and cranny sealed, every door unmovable, even the garage section where they keep their vehicles. Either the vamps lucked out, or they've been planning for the possibility of taking on the shifter estates for long enough to do a custom job on the place."

Aaron came over and leaned against the back of Marco's seat. "My kin have seen something similar near the avian estate. The vampires are prepared for a long fight. And they know the estates are the key to winning."

My pulse hiccupped. "So we can't let them break through any of those walls. We'll need all the firewood the kin can prepare, every shifter who's able to fight ready to tackle any who make it to the walls... Can we get bulletproof vests for the guards to wear? Other safety equipment? Maybe we can't use weapons ourselves, but there's no law against protecting against them, right?"

Nate frowned. "That'll only work when we stay in human form. But it couldn't hurt to have that kind of gear on hand."

Kylie perked up. "I've got an acquaintance whose brother works for a security supplies depot. He can totally hook us up."

I shook my head with a wash of relief. "Of course you know someone."

She wiggled her fingers. "I'm the most connected gal in NYC. You'd better believe it!"

All of these strategies were only stalling measures, though. "At least the vampires can't hold a real siege. We'll always have the option to scatter if the situation gets too dire, during the day when they won't know where we've gone."

"I don't think we'll keep morale very long if we abandon the estates," Aaron said. "And I can't imagine the vampires will leave a single building on them standing if we give them free access. But yes, if it comes to that..."

"And then what?" Marco said. "We scurry around through the wild as if we really are animals? We could get by like that, but it'd only be surviving. We *aren't* just animals. We need to put down roots, to have our community. And our comforts." He ran his hand over the padded arm of his seat.

"You're right. I shouldn't have suggested that." It wouldn't be the kind of victory a dragon shifter should be able to offer. I raked my fingers into my hair, my mouth twisting. "They rely on those trucks. I should have burned up some of the ones they had by the estate last night."

"Ren." Nate reached across the aisle to take my hand. He squeezed it gently, his warm brown eyes seeking out mine. "You did lots last night. So much more than any of the rest of us could manage on our own. You can't beat yourself up for that. There were too many of the vamps, and they're smart."

"But we'll find a way to beat them," Marco said. "They're contending with a fully-fledged dragon shifter and all four of her mates now." His lips curled with what looked like a genuine smile. "You've got this, princess. And we've got your back."

"We'll need to give my kin a chance to set the house in order," West said as we stepped out into the landing field.

"A bunch from the closest canine settlement got here about an hour ago to get started, but it's a big job."

The underlings he'd brought along on the plane were already hustling down the path. Only a sliver of the house's roof was visible from here. Enormous oaks and silver maples loomed between the building and our landing place.

"How long has it been since anyone's come here?" I asked. Everywhere I looked struck a new chord of recognition in me: the long stretch of the landing field, the rustling leaves of the trees, the craggy peaks of the mountains to the north that spilled down into rolling green hills that surrounded the rest of the estate. All my nerves were twanging, even though it'd only been a minute since I'd stepped off the plane.

I sucked in a breath. The breeze held the delicate floral smell of clover. That was familiar too.

"We've taken turns sending kin by to do basic upkeep over the years," Aaron said. "We didn't want the place to fall into disrepair." He rested his hand on the small of my back. "We trusted you'd be back. But it won't feel all that homey yet. They'll need to uncover the furniture, stock the kitchen, do a more thorough cleaning, all that."

I stepped toward the trees. The hiss of the breeze moving through them sent a prickle down my back. Calling to my wings.

This was where I'd first learned about being a dragon. Where I'd first seen a dragon fly. My mother, gleaming bronze against the sky. My throat choked up.

"It doesn't need any of that to feel like home," I said. "It just *is*."

I strode down the path the way the other shifters had gone. My mates drew up close behind me. I felt each of their presences by me: calm, eager, proud, and wary. And all of them here for me, trusting that I'd been right to bring us here.

I'd better make sure I justified that trust.

When we emerged from the short stretch of trees onto the plains of tall grass that surrounded the house, my breath caught in my throat. Kylie came to a halt beside me.

"Holy shit, Ren. That's some house."

It hardly even looked like a house. It was a castle, twin turrets on either side of the broad arched door, a parapet wall in between, the stones that constructed it painted stark white with red and gold trim around the door and window frames.

My mother's voice trickled up through my memory, bright with amusement. *A regular medieval fortress. Keeping us dragons safe instead of keeping the royalty safe from dragons. Our ancestor who commissioned this place had quite the sense of humor.*

These fields, I'd run through with my sisters. Ducking low to let the grass cover us, springing up to surprise each other with a mock growl. Our dads would join in the games, slinking beneath the cover of the waving blades in their animal forms, waiting to make a gentle pounce. Only my bear shifter father had been too big to really hide. We'd clamber onto his back and send him lumbering after the others.

My gaze drifted to the thicker forest behind the house. Pines and cedars mingled with oaks and maples there. The shadows streaked darker between their trunks.

But not as dark as the night when we'd fled. The air sharp in my lungs, the branches whipping against my arms, pebbles rattling away under my scrambling feet. My mother's hand clamped so tight around my fingers—

I yanked my eyes away. My heart was thudding.

"Ren?" West said, watching me. How much did he see? It hadn't occurred to me that I might not get away with quite so much around those watchful green eyes now that he was no longer trying to convince himself he didn't care.

I dragged in another breath, letting the clover smell and the summer warmth relax me. Focus on the present. Focus on the happy times before. Anything but that one night.

"I'm all right," I said. "Come on, let's get inside."

The front hall was fine. The front hall was *gorgeous*. The pale moss-green walls I'd seen in my vision now snapped into clarity. A crystal globe dangled from the ceiling, that I knew could beam with light when darkness started to fall outside. The swooping doorways opened into wide, airy rooms with huge windows that would be letting the sunlight pour in.

My feet carried me farther into the house as if of their own accord. And maybe that was my mistake. Not bracing myself. Not watching for the first hint of horror so I could pull myself back.

Or maybe there was no way I could have avoided it.

My ballet flats squeaked on the polished floor, and my stomach lurched. Like the squeak of my sisters' feet as we'd dashed this way—like the strangled squeal that had burst from Verity's throat as the rogue's jaws clamped down on her.

I whirled, trying to pull myself away from the memories, but my gaze stuck on a spot on the wall. A perfectly even green spot—they'd washed it and painted over. But I could see clear as anything where the splotch of blood had been, just beyond that door. Where it had dribbled across the floorboards to where my wolf father had slumped.

My lungs seized up. I threw myself down the hall faster. "Ren!" Kylie called out. Like my mother, in my memories. *Faster. We can't let them catch us. Oh, please, Ren, stay with me.*

A sob had choked her throat. A moan had carried behind us. One of the rogues had stepped into the hall behind us with his rifle. It all rushed at me, faster and faster: the click as he reloaded. His mocking chuckle bouncing off the walls. Another puddle of blood. The smear of fingerprints across the baseboard.

I spun again—and crashed into a broad, solid chest. Nate's arms came around me. "Ren," he murmured, dipping his head low. "I'm here. We're here. All that is over now."

I pressed my face into his shirt, but my pulse rattled on. More memories bubbled up and burst in my head. My mind was spinning. I couldn't think. I couldn't breathe.

"Let's get her to her room," West said, somewhere behind me. "There wasn't any fighting there."

"Hey." Aaron's voice, always so measured even with

its faint rasp. "Here we go, Serenity. You just need a little time to settle in. You were right. This is still your home. Hold on to that."

Was it? How could this place be mine when the rogues had painted it with my family's blood?

CHAPTER 12

Marco

I knocked on Ren's door softly, not wanting to wake her if she'd fallen asleep. When we'd brought her to the master bedroom a little more than an hour ago, she'd been shaking, her skin turned sallow. It had wrenched at me to see her so affected by this house's past, but when she'd ordered us to leave so she could collect her thoughts, she hadn't offered any room for argument.

I hoped she'd been able to let her awful memories of the attack here fade rather than falling deeper into them.

"Come in," my mate said without asking who it was. Well, she must be able to sense my presence as well as I could sense hers through the bond between us. It had only strengthened when she'd finally made that last connection with West. Good to know wolf boy wasn't completely hopeless.

Ren's voice sounded steady enough. When I eased

open the door and slipped inside, she was sitting up on her bed, on top of the covers. Her back was straight, but her face still looked paler than usual, stark in contrast with her dark brown hair. The light in her amber-brown eyes didn't hold quite the fire I'd have liked to see.

She smiled at me with just half of her mouth. I understood her well enough by now to read what she was feeling then. She was embarrassed by how she'd broken down. As if any of us who'd been with her when she'd gotten overwhelmed would judge her for it.

I ambled over to the bed as if nothing at all were amiss and sat down at the foot, reaching to take her hand. "How is my Princess of Flames?"

She scooted closer. "Not feeling very regal," she muttered. "I'm not going to accomplish whatever I'm supposed to do here if I can't walk down the hall without getting buried in memories."

"They'll fade," I said, stroking my thumb over the back of her hand. "It's your first time back here. Of course they hit you hard. I have no doubt you'll be back to your usual regal ass-kicking self in no time."

She gave me a fuller smile at that remark, but her eyes still looked a little weary.

"Is something else bothering you, princess?" I asked.

She leaned her head against my shoulder. My whole body lit up in an instant, with desire and affection. A week ago, she might have hesitated to get even this close with me. The fact that she was now my mate in every possible way felt almost miraculous.

I was very much looking forward to experiencing that miracle again and again.

For now, I suspected affection was going to be more what she needed than desire. I slipped my arm around her waist, and she sighed.

"The way the memories hit me, how much they shook me up... I'm just worrying about all the kin waiting for us back on the other estates," she said. "I thought I was going to find answers here. What if the past has clouded my mind too much to see where I have to go?"

"There are only so many doors in this place, big as it is," I pointed out. "I'm sure we can manage to find the one."

"The vampires could attack again in just a few hours. We don't have much time."

I pulled her closer to me. "Our kin fended them off before. The strategy you came up with is sound—and it worked just fine in the places that didn't have a dragon shifter on hand last night."

She rubbed her mouth, frowning. "It won't be enough if the vampires keep at us. There are ways of getting past regular fire, putting it out... I wish I could be everywhere at once. Burn them all up. Just *end* this."

Oh, my dear mate. I dipped my head to kiss her temple. "It's been a long, hard journey here, hasn't it? You deserved a much more peaceful welcome."

"Maybe I didn't. There was nothing peaceful about how I left." Her laugh sounded a bit choked. She twined her fingers with mine, looking down at our joined hands. Her voice dropped. "It felt so good for a little while there. Having my bond confirmed with all of you. Like everything had fallen into exactly the right place. But now I can't help thinking about how easily I could lose all of that."

The last four alphas had fallen here too. This was where her mother had lost her mates and Ren her fathers.

Ren's other hand drifted to her belly, so instinctively I wondered if she even noticed the motion. How much of her fear was the echo of the little girl she'd been—and how much the connection to the dragon shifter who'd come before her, who'd lost children and mates? Who'd lost *everything* to save Ren.

Some of both, I thought. All tangled up together. Maybe my mate needed more than affection after all. She needed to feel every bit of her power—the power she held inside her, and the power we generated between us.

I tugged her onto her feet. A full-length mirror, the glass bright within its ornate gold frame, stood against the wall across from her wardrobes. I guided her over to it. She raised an eyebrow at me.

"Trying to distract me with the horror of my bedhead?"

I chuckled. "No. Just look at yourself."

I stood behind her as she gazed into the mirror, my hands resting on her waist. Her hair wasn't actually all that mussed, falling in its loose waves halfway down her back. The casual dress she'd picked hugged her curves gently, but no less appealingly than if it'd been a silk gown.

"That's not just a princess looking back at you," I said, holding her gaze in the mirror from over her shoulder. "That's a queen. A queen who's taken every bit of bullshit anyone's thrown at her and soared above it all."

"Yeah?" she said.

"Oh, yeah. Look at those eyes. I've loved the fire in them since the first moment I saw you. That was all I needed for me to know you had it in you to take on whatever the world threw at you." I swept the fall of her hair to the side so I could kiss the crook of her jaw. "And that stubborn mouth. Never letting anyone off the hook—unless they deserve a second chance. Because a queen knows when to be merciful too."

I brushed my thumb over her soft lips. Ren's eyes glimmered. She let her lips part, teasing the edge of her teeth against my thumb. Just like that, I was hard.

I ran my fingers over her arms next, down to the sensitive skin inside her elbows. "The strength in you, anyone can see it. Never backing down from a challenge. Always ready to defend your kin."

My hands slipped beneath her arms and up her torso to trace the undersides of her breasts. Ren's breath hitched, her eyelids dipping. "And I haven't even mentioned how fucking gorgeous you are. I could look at nothing but you for days and still be enjoying the view."

"Go on," she said, her voice roughening. The color was coming back into her cheeks, a lovely rosy flush. I kissed my way down the side of her neck to her shoulder. My hands rose to completely cup her breasts. She leaned back against me as I stroked the peaks, making her nipples pebble against the fabric of her dress. Heat radiated between us.

"We both know how much passion you've got in this beautiful body," I murmured by her ear. "Keep watching. See what a woman you are."

Ren

I shivered with pleasure as Marco continued to caress my breasts. Each flick over my nipples sent a fresh quiver of electric bliss through my body. And somehow seeing it in the mirror—the rising flush in my cheeks and neck, his lithe fingers working over my curves through the dress—turned me on even more.

I watched him lower his head a second before his mouth found my earlobe. He gave it a light nip that made me gasp. When his eye met mine again, they were hooded and dark with his own passion.

Marco's hand trailed down my side to the hem of my dress, just past my thighs. I pressed back into him instinctively, my ass brushing his cock, already at attention in his slacks. An even deeper tremor ran through me—and a knock sounded on my door.

Aaron's voice carried through. "Serenity?"

My mind was so muddled with desire an answer popped out automatically. "Come in."

Marco arched his eyebrows at me in the mirror. Oh. Er... But Aaron was already stepping inside.

He stopped on the threshold of the bedroom, the door thudding shut behind him. His bright gaze took in the scene: Marco and me standing together in front of the mirror, my cheeks pink and nipples poking against the fabric of my dress, one of the feline alpha's hands still molded over my breast. I could almost feel the thump of

Aaron's heart speeding up, the heat emanating from his skin at the sight of us.

"If I'm interrupting something..." the eagle shifter said, his tone mild even though his eyes had lit with interest.

Marco shifted a little to one side, dipping to kiss the other side of my neck, as if to indicate there was plenty of room to share. My pulse raced a little faster. Of course it didn't matter if another of my mates saw us. He could join us.

"Definitely not," I said, a little breathless. "At least not if you want to stay."

The eager sound he made in his throat seemed to answer that question. Aaron crossed the space between us in an instant, sliding his arm around my waist.

I turned my head to kiss him. As the avian alpha captured my mouth, Marco slicked his tongue up my neck. Heat flooded me from both sides. Aaron teased his thumb over one breast as Marco continued to fondle the other. My panties had already dampened, but I had the feeling they were soaking now.

I reached up to curl my fingers into both of their shirts. No, that wasn't what I wanted to be feeling. I jerked at the collars. Aaron smiled against my mouth. He gave me one last kiss, tilting his head to deepen it. Then he eased back just enough to pull his thin polo over his head.

Marco followed suit, undoing the first two buttons of his linen dress shirt and then yanking the whole thing off, rumpling his jagged black hair. I glanced over at him, wanting to see him beside me and not just in the mirror.

My fingers traced over the fading scars in his tan skin where the tiger shifter who'd challenged him had wounded him. I kissed one mark on his shoulder, another on his jaw, then brought his mouth to mine.

Marco kissed me hard and hungry. His eyes gleamed when he pulled back. His fingers gripped the hem of my dress insistently. Aaron grasped the other side, and they pulled the cotton sundress off together.

The avian alpha immediately bent to suck my bare nipple into his mouth. His steady hand caressed the curve of my ass. Marco claimed my lips again, his hand slipping between us. I trembled as his fingers glided over my sex to the nub of my clit. Pleasure sparked from my core. I moaned against his mouth.

Marco's thumb swiveled over my clit, drawing another whimper from me. Then he yanked my panties down and slid his fingers down over my hot, slick opening. My hips canted toward him of their own accord. Yes. Yes, *please*. I clutched the hem of his slacks with a determined tug. He chuckled and eased back to chuck them off.

Aaron took the opportunity to trail his lips down my body until he reached my sex. I gasped as he pressed his mouth to my core. The tips of his teeth grazed over my clit, and a full-out cry broke from my throat. I rocked into his touch, needing more.

Marco brought his body up against mine from behind again. His hands slipped over my hips. The hard length of his cock rubbed over my ass and between my legs. I edged my feet apart to give him better access, tipping forward to rest my hands on the mirror's frame.

Aaron kissed the planes of my stomach as the jaguar shifter nudged my opening with the head of his cock. Marco pressed forward, and I whimpered as the solid length of him penetrated me. "Fuck, princess," he muttered, his fingers tightening around my hips. "You're the best thing I've ever felt."

He drew back and plunged in even deeper, sending a rush of bliss through my nerves. Aaron ducked back down to lave my clit. My body swayed with each of Marco's thrusts, pressing my mound to Aaron's mouth. He rocked with us, gripping my thigh, his tongue swirling over my nub until I was outright shaking with the rising pleasure.

"Look," Marco murmured, leaning over me as he adjusted his angle. I moaned, bucking faster to meet his pace, chasing that peak of bliss I'd almost reached. At the same time, I lifted my gaze.

My reflection looked back at me, flushed and wild. I'd never seen my eyes so bright with emotion before. Emotion and power. I had one man groaning against my shoulder as his hips jerked to meet me, another devouring my sex from the outside. Aaron's golden head didn't miss a beat as he unzipped his jeans to stroke his cock in time with our love-making.

He nipped my clit, and Marco thrust even harder. Ecstasy swept through me. I shattered between them with a sharp cry, my hand dropping to squeeze Aaron's shoulder. Marco's breath shuddered against my skin as my pussy squeezed tight around his cock. He spilled himself into me. Aaron groaned at the same time, giving me one last swipe of his tongue as he spent himself in his hand.

I stayed there between my mates as the crash of pleasure ebbed, my legs shaking. Aaron let me hold onto him. He pressed a tender kiss to my inner thigh. Marco hummed happily as he softened inside me, and nuzzled my shoulder.

I looked at the wild, sated woman in the mirror—a woman who had claimed her four mates. A woman who'd overcome rogues and fae. Yes, that was who I was now. The tragedies of years ago didn't matter, not when it came to fulfilling my role.

I wasn't that little girl anymore. I was a woman. I was the dragon shifter. And I *would* unearth whatever secrets my estate was keeping hidden.

Ren

A COUPLE of West's kin had already gotten to work in the kitchens, which was a good thing. None of us had eaten anything resembling lunch, just a few snacks that'd been stashed on the plane. Feeling a lot more grounded than I had when I'd first walked into the house, I ambled into the dining area, found a platter of stuffed rolls ready and waiting, and grabbed one to chow down on while I wandered farther.

My memories hadn't faded completely. Now and then my eyes twitched to a doorway a rogue had left from, a spot where I'd heard an agonized cry. But my mind didn't spin off into the past like it had before. I focused on the firm floor behind my feet and the heady warmth of the bonds between my mates and me. It seemed to have grown even more solid during that interlude with Marco and Aaron.

The strength in this body and the strength of those bonds held me here in the present. I had so much more to do here. Maybe a victory against the vampires wouldn't make up for what had happened in the past, but I could hope that victory would send us toward a much brighter future.

The rooms in the east wing were all familiar. I'd spent most of my time in those when we'd been living here—when I wasn't roaming around outside. When I entered the west side of the house, a prickle ran down my back.

Mom had taken me this way a couple times to show me something she was working on. But mostly we'd steered clear. It had been her domain as the ruling dragon shifter.

I swallowed the rest of the sandwich and treaded farther down that hall. *I* was the ruling dragon shifter now.

I wasn't expecting to hear a patter of footsteps coming toward me. Kylie hustled around a bend, her face lighting up when she saw me. "Ren!" She twisted her hands in front of her with a slightly guilty expression. "I know you're exploring this place on your own, but I couldn't help being curious... I found a door like the one you described, the one from your vision. Do you want to, like, find it on your own or is it okay for me to show you?"

Trust Kylie to have already scoped the whole place out.

"It's fine," I said with a grin. "Lead the way."

Whatever I found here, I didn't know if I was meant to face it alone. I'd rather have my mates by my side. As

Kylie beckoned me down the hall she'd emerged from, I focused on the warm pulse of the bond inside me. I knew where each of my alphas were, approximately. And I discovered, testing the feel of our connection, that I could give them all a tug. *Come here.*

That was handy. I'd have to remember that trick. Nate had told me that eventually I'd be able to sense whenever he or the others were in pain, even across a long distance. Being able to give them a nudge in my direction must be part of that increased awareness.

The hall Kylie had explored took us around to the back corner of the house. She stopped in front of the door. And it was The Door. They were all the same moss green, but this one had that circle of dimples just above my line of sight. And no handle, no knob. But just like in my vision, I knew, looking at it, I could open it easily.

Heavier footsteps sounded down the hall. All four of my mates came into view. They must have caught up with each other on the way over.

"This is it?" Aaron asked, inspecting the door as they joined me.

I nodded. "I haven't tried to open it yet."

"Well, what are you waiting for, Sparks?" West said. His tone was more teasing than gruff. "This is what we came all this way for."

Nate eased closer as if to offer his help, but I could feel down to my bones that this task was only mine. I drew in my breath and stepped up to the door. My hands rose as if summoned to rest on either side of the dimpled circle.

A shiver of energy raced down my arms. A burning

sensation crept up my throat, as if I were kindling dragon fire in my human form. I paused, and then exhaled in a steady stream against the circle.

No fire burst from my lips, only a rush of air. But the door twitched and swung open, away from my hands.

On the other side, a straight, narrow staircase led down into a basement room. A soft glow crept into the space below as I watched. I hadn't realized this house even had a basement. I stared at the staircase for a second, anticipation tingling over my skin.

"You've got this, princess," Marco said.

I did. I moved forward, down one step and the next, my fingers trailing along the smooth wall. The tingling sensation washed over me even more deeply, with one very clear impression.

Whatever was waiting for me below, it was only for me.

"I don't think you can come with me," I said to the guys and Kylie behind me.

"Nope," Marco agreed. "Couldn't even if we tried. That place doesn't want us at all."

"I've never felt anything like that before," Aaron murmured, mostly to himself, with awed curiosity.

"You just holler if you need us, then," Kylie said.

I walked further, down into the room. The door clicked shut behind me. The air pressure thickened, as if to embrace me. My feet hit the tiled floor at the bottom, and a fresh breath rushed into my lungs with a cool, powdery smell.

I was here.

And where was *here*, exactly? I rotated slowly, taking in the whole room.

The space was lined with shelves, and each of them held a row of glinting slabs. I stepped closer. They were crystal tablets, like the one Mom had left for me in the abandoned subway tunnel that had led us to Sunridge—and to my new fiery power to get at the truth.

The room was packed with them, all of them etched with one or more symbols, many of which didn't mean anything to me. The only other objects the room contained were an armchair with a high arched back and a small rosewood side table.

The place felt like a library, if you could read crystals instead of books. But then, Mom had managed to leave me a message in that first crystal. The truth-seeking flames and a vision of my mother's murder had been contained in a larger crystal. Who knew what any of these might hold?

I had no idea where to start, so I grabbed one at random. A quiver of energy raced across my palms. The etching on this one showed what looked vaguely like a bear standing on its hind legs between a horse and a weasel. Interesting.

I sank into the chair. Instinct told me to press the crystal tablet to my chest. An odd warmth bled from its smooth surface into my skin. Then a clear, even voice started speaking in my head.

"Dragon shifter Matilde, May 2, 1876. I record this history of a conflict resolved among the disparate kin."

As the long-gone dragon shifter's words rolled into my mind, a vision formed before my eyes, like the glimpse

I'd gotten of my mother's death. But I got the sense this one was more symbolic than any literal event. A tall woman with sleek black hair stood with a burly man next to her, in a yard I vaguely recognized from the disparate estate. Several shifters in animal form prowled on either side of the pair.

"For five years, my alphas and I have seen a growing hostility between the meat-eating and plant-eating members of the disparate kin. Accusations of wrongdoing have been thrown from both sides. A few skirmishes have resulted in many injured and four dead. The primary point of contention appeared to be—"

I pulled the crystal away from my chest and set it on the side table, breaking the vision and the voice. With a couple of slow breaths, I settled back into the present. My gaze skimmed the shelves again.

So these were histories? Records committed to the crystals by the dragon shifters before me—reports they hoped later dragon shifters would find useful?

I hadn't seen any conflicts among the disparate kin while I'd been there, and Nate hadn't mentioned any. That record might be worthwhile to listen to later, but for now, it wasn't what I needed.

I stood up, slid that crystal back onto its shelf, and considered the others. There were hundreds in this room. Which one would give me something I could use against the vampires?

No way to find out but through trial and error.

The tablets clinked softly as I flipped through several on the shelf at head height, peering at the images etched on them. Those clearly gave some idea as to the contents.

How would you draw a vampire? A stick figure with little triangles jutting from its mouth?

An artist I was not. God, would I be recording the trials I'd experienced over the last few weeks on one of these crystals when all this trouble was over?

I pushed that thought aside and bent to look through the next shelf. My hand stilled over a tablet with a few sketchy human-ish figures on left and a wolf, lion, and eagle on the right. Those first figures could be vampires, maybe?

Worth a try. I picked it up and got comfy on the armchair again.

The voice that spilled into my head when I held this tablet close was huskier, more abrupt. "Dragon shifter Geraldine, November 14, 1937. I chronicle the current state of shifter-human interactions. I've been watching this problem get worse since I was a little girl. The humans keep breeding, and more of them keep pouring in from across the ocean. Their cities are expanding. They set down new roots anywhere they please. Sometimes far too close to our shifter territories than is really comfortable."

The image that swam up before my eyes showed a group of shifters watching houses being erected up the hillside from their village. It morphed into a scene of the same shifters loading up cars with boxes from their houses, then driving off down a winding road, deeper into the wilderness.

"We have preserved the lands around our estates for centuries, but those who want to live elsewhere are finding their options increasingly limited by the number and distribution of human communities. I'll now go into detail about some of the strategies we've used to limit exposure between—"

I removed the tablet and gave my head a quick shake to clear it. The information my ancestor had been relating there was stuff I'd definitely want to come back to—but not right now, when vampires were causing us a hell of a lot more trouble than any humans.

A couple of the shelves were empty, I guessed to make room for future contributions. I left the human occupation tablet on one of those so I could find it again easily when I had time to really pay attention.

A glance into a closed cabinet revealed stacks of blank crystals that must have been for my or later dragon shifter's use. Hopefully there was an instruction manual around here somewhere. I returned to pawing through the other records.

Partway through the next row, an etching caught my eye with a pang of recognition. I pulled out that tablet.

On closer examination, the image wasn't exactly the same as the one I'd remembered. It showed dragons and humanoid figures a little too tall and slim to be really human. The fae. I'd seen carvings like this on the pedestal in the mountain caves, where I'd found the truth-seeking flames that fae and shifter magic had created together.

Dragons and fae stood together in the picture on the tablet too. One fae figure had its hand resting on the shoulder of the dragon beside it. Two others stood with their heads bent toward each other, a shape like a flame between them.

It didn't look like this one would say anything about vampires, but then, maybe our relations with the other dominant paranormal community would give me some insight. And I couldn't deny I was curious how we and those wispy, shimmering beings had ever gotten along.

I took my spot on the chair again and clasped the tablet to my chest.

"Dragon shifter Charlotte, 1842. I would like to record a joint project I've embarked on with our fae companions, and to detail the current state of our alliance."

An alliance, huh? That had obviously fallen apart a long time ago.

I managed not to tense up as this tablet's vision spilled out before my eyes. Tall, slim, shining fae were flitting through an open forest amid a pack of wolves. A dragon, emerald green, soared by overhead.

The fae weren't fleeing the shifters or chasing them. I could tell from the flashes of smiles and the way they wove between each other's groups that they were... *enjoying* sharing the woods. Not an image I'd ever expected to see.

But then, the only time I'd seen more than one fae at a time was in the vision that had showed a bunch of them killing my mother with their magic.

"I suppose it makes sense that we shifters and the fae can understand each other better than either of us relates to the vampires," the former dragon shifter's sweet voice continued. "Unlike them, we are both drawn to life more so than death. While some of us may enjoy a night-time run, every shifter I've ever met enjoys a good lie-about in the sun, which the fae worship. And my dragon fire has so much in common with fae magic, they assure me we can link the two together, their power sharing mine. I'm excited by the possibilities."

The image whirled around to show the emerald dragon breathing fire toward a fae woman—who was encompassing it in a stream of her own blue-ish magic. My breath caught, watching it. I eased the tablet away from me to get my bearings.

Blue and red, mingling together. To create the violet of my truth-seeking flames? Had this dragon shifter been the one to create the power I'd stumbled on nearly two centuries later?

If we'd managed to create *that* power with the fae, what else might we be capable of together?

As soon as the question passed through my head, my throat tightened. Maybe the dragon shifters had been able to work alongside the fae in the distant past, but a lot had changed since then. How had we come to the point where the fae monarch would look the other way while her people slaughtered my mother?

How the hell could we ever trust them again?

I didn't know what had gone wrong, but I couldn't answer any of those questions without knowing more. Inhaling deeply, I brought the tablet back to my chest to see what else my long-ago ancestor could tell me.

CHAPTER 14

Ren

My name reached me as if from a huge distance away, across an ocean maybe. At first I almost didn't hear it. Then it penetrated my focus even more insistently.

"Ren! Princess, if you don't say something soon, I'm going to have to start clanging the sirens."

I jerked the tablet I'd been clutching away from my chest. My head spun. My stomach pinched, deep into the hollow it had formed in my belly.

How long had I been down here in the basement archive? I rubbed my forehead as if that would clear the mugginess around my thoughts and finally found the wherewithal to answer Marco. "I'm here! Sorry. I just got... really absorbed."

His chuckled carried, muted, down the stairs. "You might want to consider getting unabsorbed for a bit. I'm thinking it's about time you ate something.

And while *I* have full confidence in your ability to look after yourself, some of your other mates may be wearing holes in the carpet with their pacing up here."

I had been down here longer than I realized, then. That pinching in my stomach was a reminder that yes, at some point I should have dinner.

I pushed myself off the armchair. The muscles in my back twanged from so much time spent sitting. Sitting and gazing into visions of times past.

But I still hadn't found what I was looking for. Not the reason we'd fallen out with the fae. Not a reason to think we could ever count on them again. I bit my lip, nibbling at it in my frustration, as I climbed back up to the main floor.

Marco had stepped back from the doorway to let me through. "There's my dragon shifter," he said lightly. "Did you find anything useful?"

"I don't know," I said. The climb had left me dizzy. This belly needed food ASAP. "It'd probably be better if I talk about it with all of you at once."

"I can summon a little patience."

He paused, giving me a once-over. I guess I looked about as rough as I felt. The feline alpha's expression softened. He cupped my face, cradling my jaw, and pressed a butterfly of a kiss to the middle of my forehead. "If you're not there yet, you will be soon, princess. I'm sure of that."

Good. Someone really should be, and it sure as hell wasn't me.

The hearty smell of freshly grilled steaks reached my

nose. By the time we arrived at the dining room, my mouth was full of saliva.

"Look what the cat dragged in," Marco announced with a smirk as the other alphas glanced up where they were standing around the table.

Kylie was there too. She bounded over first. "So what's the big secret? Can you even tell us what's down there? What have you been doing all afternoon?"

Everyone's eyes trained on me. Waiting to hear that this trip had been worthwhile. My gut knotted. "It's... kind of hard to explain."

Marco rested his hands on my shoulder. "I think our Princess of Flames needs to get some nourishment into her. Where's that dinner?"

As if on cue, a couple of the kin emerged from the kitchen then, carrying plates. Nate motioned for them to give the first one to me. I dropped into the nearest chair and grabbed the waiting cutlery.

It only took a couple of bites before my head started to clear. I gulped water from the glass someone had brought me and looked around the table. My alphas and Kylie were all eating, the rest of the kin having left us some privacy.

But their attention was still on me. As soon as my hands stilled, West looked up, catching my gaze with a question in his. Aaron raised his head, his own eyes glinting with enthusiasm. He must have been dying to know what dragon shifter secrets I'd discovered.

Nothing down in that archive felt all that top secret. I had the feeling no one except the dragon shifters was meant to go down there and handle the tablets directly, but nothing about them told me I shouldn't share the information I'd learned.

The hard part was figuring out how to explain all that information without the helpful murmur of a voice in my ear and mental images for illustration.

"I haven't found out anything specific about the vampires," I said slowly. "There's—it's basically a records room. Pieces of history past dragon shifters saved for the ones who came later, about what happened in the past. I ended up spending most of the time on records about the fae."

West's eyes narrowed. "How do they fit in? Do you think they're helping the vampires?"

"No, not at all," I said, waving my hand as if that gesture would dispel any wrong impressions I'd given. "One thing I know from what I've heard is there's *no* way the fae would ever ally with the vampires. They're pretty much opposites. But I guess you all already know that."

I rubbed my face. In so many areas, I was still just catching up to basic paranormal knowledge. There was one thing they didn't know much about, though. "I was more interested in the ways they used to work with the shifters."

"So the records talked more about that association?" Aaron leaned forward. "I don't know why our own histories are so sparse on that subject."

"It seems like the fae leaders mostly preferred to deal with the dragon shifters," I said. "Something about... feeling the closest kinship with us, because they're all about light and energy, and that's kind of the same as our fire? So I don't get the impression they interacted with the other shifters a whole lot even back then."

"And better for us that they didn't," West muttered.

I hesitated. I knew better than maybe anyone here what a sensitive subject this was for him. "They were *good* allies, at least in some ways, back then," I had to say. "It's thanks to them and one of the past dragon shifters that I've been able to draw the truth out of our enemies. They created that power so it would be ready when there was a time of great need... It took them *years* to perfect it and contain it. The fae didn't get anything out of that effort except knowing they'd given us a new strength."

"That and a handy way to tempt shifters up the mountain where they could pick us off," Marco pointed out.

I glowered at him. "That obviously wasn't the original plan."

"What was the plan?" Nate asked in his low baritone. "Why did they think someone would need that power? Why not give it to the dragon shifter already there?"

"I guess that dragon shifter didn't need it. The impression I get is that it was, like, an ace for us to have up our sleeve. Seeing how quickly the world was starting to change, how much territory humans were claiming here... Little did they know it'd be partly our own people causing the chaos." I grimaced. "But that's not the point."

"Something about this alliance seems meaningful to you right now," Aaron prompted, his gaze intent on me. "Why did you focus on that thread of our history?"

"Partly I just happened to stumble on it. And after that... I get the sense that it's all tied together somehow.

The relationships between the different paranormal communities. The way we've clashed. I can't pin it down yet, but I feel like there's *something* important in all those past events that might help us see what to do." I paused and sighed. "And also I haven't come across many records about vampires at all. It seems like we've mostly steered clear of each other."

"That sounds accurate," Marco said. "If only they'd keep steering clear."

"If there's anything to learn about the fae, it's that they're backstabbing bastards," West broke in. "Maybe they pretended to ally with us before, but everything they've done since..." He swept his arm through the air in a violent motion that made me think of his mottled scar. "You follow whatever paths you want, Sparks, but I can't see us gaining anything from the fae we're dealing with now."

The twist of his mouth echoed how I felt, thinking about the fae. They'd taken both of our mothers from us, hadn't they? I swallowed hard and reached across the table to touch his hand.

A day or two ago, I'd have expected him to jerk his arm away. Funny how much one conversation—and, er, other activities following said conversation—could change things. He turned his hand so I could twine my fingers through his.

"I know," I said. "Believe me, I don't trust them either." But even as I said those words, a deeper discomfort echoed through me. The way that past dragon shifter had talked about the fae, warmly, almost admiring...

Had she really been completely deceived, or was there more to the fae than I'd been able to see in my own experiences?

"What do we do now?" Kylie asked.

I frowned. "I don't know." My gaze slid to the window. It had darkened into evening outside. "Has there been any word from the estates or any of the other communities?"

Nate shook his head. "I gave my kin instructions to contact me as soon as there was any news. I'll be keeping my phone right by me."

"Same as all of us," Marco said. "And when we hear anything, you'll be the first to know, Ren."

Were the vampires really going to hold off on us tonight? I found that hard to believe. Some part of me had felt I needed to come here. I *had* to figure out why.

I gave West's hand a quick squeeze before letting go and reaching for my fork. "I guess the best plan I have is to get some more dinner in me, and then go back to the records room. There's got to be something useful down there."

The soft glow of the crystals was starting to sting my eyes. I leaned against the side of the armchair and rubbed them. The meal had revived my energy for a few hours, but I could feel myself flagging again. The last few tablets I'd taken out, more out of desperation than any clear sign they'd be useful, hadn't given me any real guidance.

There had to be something more about the fae. How

could we have fallen apart to the point of becoming almost enemies without any dragon shifter recording those events? They're reported on the freaking crop growth patterns, for fuck's sake.

I'd just straightened up to roll the cricks out of my shoulders when my gaze snagged on a glinting corner just barely protruding between two of the shelving units. Kneeling beside them, I slid my hand in and tugged. One, and then another, and then another tablet tumbled out. They must have fallen through a gap in the partly open sides of the shelves and gotten wedged back there.

As I examined my new finds, my pulse fluttered. One of them showed a fae figure and a dragon on either side of a jagged line. I didn't need to be a psychoanalyst to take a stab at what that might mean.

I shoved the other two tablets onto a shelf and dropped into the chair. Time to find out what the hell had gone wrong between us and the fae.

"Dragon shifter Mirabel," a weary voice said. "1908. It is with sad heart that I report the dissolution of our friendly relations with fae kind. An accident was made on our part, I'll admit that, but they've proven completely unwilling to listen to reason."

The images rose up and faded from one to another before my eyes. Humans settling near one of the shifter villages. One of them killing a partridge shifter who'd gone out to stretch her wings. The shifters gathering their things and moving deeper into the nearby wilderness. "Fae territory," Mirabel said. "But they had shared with us before. And my kin had little choice of where to go."

But the scene before me went wrong. The shifters

hustled the carts packed with their belongings along through the sparsely wooded plains and sent them careening down a hill without seeing the small group of fae who'd been relaxing below. The fae shrieked and scattered, but one didn't leap up quite in time. A cart's wheel slammed right over his leg.

I flinched, watching. The fae boy scrambled away, dragging his wounded leg, his face twisted with agony. One of his companions gave a shout and hurled a bolt of magic at the cart. It split in two with a sizzle, half the cargo bursting into shimmers of light.

Precious belongings, all the shifters had left from their own home. My long-ago kin let out a wail. One of them lunged at the fae who'd cast the magic, knocking her to the ground with a slash of talons. Then the image faded.

"So naturally I was called in to resolve the conflict," the dragon shifter said. "I went to see the fae monarch to resolve the situation peacefully. But she was not happy to see only me. She wished for my kin to be brought before her for her judgment. As if she didn't trust my own. I couldn't leave my kin to that potential vengeance. But she took my refusal as a horrific insult. Wouldn't hear any talk of compensation for *my* kin's losses."

The fae queen in the vision spun on her heel, a cloud of magic gusting between her and Mirabel. The dragon shifter strode off in the other direction.

"They've been cold to us ever since," she said in my mind. "Driving us from lands we once shared. Refusing assistance to kin in need. The way they're behaving, I can't help but wonder if they've been simply waiting for a moment such as this as an excuse to set themselves apart from us. My mother said they once tried to steal her fire. Maybe they've realized we'll never permit that, and we're no longer of any use to them. Good riddance, in that case."

Her voice faded away. I came back to the records room, clutching the tablet. My heart was thudding.

Was that really how the animosity between our peoples had started? With a simple accident and a kneejerk act of retaliation. But I guessed tensions had been building for some time underneath, if the previous dragon shifter had suspected the fae... of trying to *steal* her fire? What the hell did that even mean?

And how did you get from there to outright murder?

CHAPTER 15

Nate

I DIDN'T KNOW what time it was, but the moon was stark against the black sky outside my window. I shoved myself out of bed and checked the phone on my room's desk again, as if I'd have missed it if someone had called or texted. No alerts, of course.

I grimaced at the screen and walked into the ensuite bathroom. Tiny aches still nibbled at my muscles here and there if I moved at any speed. I could pretend to be totally recovered, but inside the holes the bullets had dug weren't quite finished healing.

My body had better hurry up and stitch itself whole. There was too much fighting still ahead of us.

The brief walk didn't leave me any more ready to sleep. My head was muggy, but the rest of me was on high alert. Any moment, that call announcing disaster might come. Any moment, Ren might need me.

I tossed myself back into bed anyway, burrowing my face in the pillow. I'd be a lot more useful to all of them if I wasn't a zombie from exhaustion.

The blanket cocooned me in warmth. Crickets chirped beyond the window. The aches faded from my muscles. But I still couldn't quite drift off.

The door to my rooms eased open, a faint click and a whisper of air. Quiet footsteps padded across the floor. I caught my mate's familiar scent before she'd made it halfway across the bedroom. My eyes opened, and she shot me a soft smile. I pushed myself over on the bed to make more room for her.

She clambered right up and slid under the covers, wrapping her arm around me. I slept in nothing but boxers. The feel of her bare skin against mine set my nerves on alert in a much more gratifying way.

"Finished your researching?" I asked.

"For now, anyway." Ren nestled her head under my chin and pressed a kiss to my shoulder. "Everyone else is already asleep. I wanted someone to cuddle up with. And I thought you might be feeling a little neglected."

I snorted. "I'm sure you were giving me plenty of attention while I was out of commission. It's not your fault I wasn't conscious enough to enjoy it."

She made a humming sound and squirmed even closer. I definitely wasn't going to complain about the attention now.

"How are you feeling now?" she asked. "Still sore?"

I didn't want her fretting about me, but I wasn't going to lie to her. "A little. When you're injured that badly, it takes a while for everything to sort itself out. But I'm almost there." I ran my hand over her hair. "You must still be feeling that attack last night."

She shrugged. "It's not so bad. I've spent most of the day sitting in one chair or another. Plenty of rest." She tipped her head back to look me in the eyes. "I'm sure you need *your* rest. You came out of that coma less than a day ago. I hope I didn't wake you up."

"No, I've been doing a good job of keeping myself awake all by myself," I said with a half-smile.

Her brow knit. "Worrying about your kin?"

"Mostly. It's hard not to. But I think I'll have an easier time letting go of those thoughts with you here."

"Hmm." She teased her hand up my neck and urged my head down. I met her lips with a long, gentle kiss. My body reacted instantly, heat washing through me, my cock thickening. By the time our mouths slipped apart, I was painfully hard and not minding it at all.

"You know," Ren said, a mischievous note coming into her voice, "I remember a time not all that long ago when I was all tensed up with worries, and you found the perfect way to relax me."

An eager quiver ran through me. "I'm all for that."

I moved to cover her body with mine, but she held me back with a light press of her hand. "No," she murmured, letting her fingers slip down my chest and abdomen to the waist of my boxers. "I was thinking of that first time, in the van... I don't want you straining anything that's not quite healed. You just relax and let me take care of you."

Dear God, when she said it like that, looking at me through her eyelashes so coyly, I just about came apart from that alone.

Ren pulled me into another kiss, this one more intense, while her hand ventured under my boxers. I groaned as her fingers closed around my erection. She stroked me loosely at first, and then with firming grip, her thumb flicking over the head of my cock. Pleasure shot through my veins.

I kissed her harder, but that wasn't enough. Even if she wouldn't let me respond with all the passion I wanted to give her, I could still share this bliss. As I rocked into her grasp, I reached up under her dress and tucked my hand between her legs.

Ren whimpered. Our kisses turned sloppier as we both began to pant. I rubbed the heel of my hand against her clit, my fingers testing and then dipping inside her opening. She slicked precum down my length and pumped me faster.

I was soaring on pleasure now. Was this how it felt when she shifted into that magnificent dragon form and sailed up into the sky?

The pressure building in my balls was the most amazing torture, but I wanted to see her through first. I hooked my fingers higher into the tight, hot center of her. She gasped. My thumb pressed down on her nub, and her sex clenched around me. She shuddered with a broken sound of ecstasy, but her hold on me didn't falter. Two more steady strokes, and I was spilling over with her.

We sagged deeper into the mattress, our breaths falling back into an easier rhythm together. Ren kissed me one more time, so perfectly sweet. And perfectly right. As she snuggled against me again, my body finally let go of the last of its tensions, and I drifted into sleep.

Ren

When I woke up next to Nate, my eyelids protested, too heavy to comfortably lift. I blinked blearily at the dark room. It was still night outside the window.

But a tremor of unease had passed over me. My pulse was thumping faster.

Something was wrong. My mates were upset.

I tried to slip out from under the blanket without waking Nate, but he stirred as soon as I moved. "Ren?" he murmured.

"I just want to make sure everything's all right," I said. "You can stay right there."

Fat chance of that. The bear shifter shoved back the blankets to join me. He grabbed a housecoat from a hook on his wardrobe. My dress was wrinkled, but I didn't really care. Everyone in this house had seen me looking a lot worse.

We came out into the hall to find West striding toward us. He stopped, taking in the two of us with a twitch of amusement at the corner of his mouth. Otherwise his expression was grim. My stomach balled tighter.

"I was just coming to get both of you," he said. "Looks like it's an easy job."

He turned to head back the way he'd come with a motion for us to follow. I caught up with him. "What's going on?" I said. "Have the vampires made another attack?"

"Of course they have," he muttered, his voice as grim as his face. "They've been experimenting with different tactics to counteract the fires. Water tanks with hoses to spray them down, mostly. Around the estates our kin added extra gasoline to the wood so it wouldn't burn out so easily, but there were a couple of villages hit that hadn't evacuated... They weren't prepared enough."

My heart sank. "Did anyone make it out?"

He shook his head, his jaw clenched. Behind me, Nate swore. "None of my lieutenants have contacted me."

"They might still be busy fighting the vamps off," I pointed out. And no matter what was happening out there, there was nothing he or the rest of us could do about it right now. By the time we made it to any village, it'd be morning, the vampires gone—and whatever wreckage they'd left behind already settled.

"That's not all," West said as we strode into the private common room meant for just the five of us. "I had a couple of my people watching the only highway that comes close to this estate. A truck stinking of vamps passed by not long ago, heading our way. Maybe they're hoping they'll catch us by surprise, coming this deep into our territory, like the rogues did before. The speed they were going, they'll be here in the next half hour."

My pulse stuttered. "We haven't put up any defenses." The dragon shifter estate boasted a stone wall around its inner boundaries much like the one at the canine estate, but that wouldn't stop the vampires by itself. We hadn't brought enough kin with us to fully defend it. We hadn't laid down wood for a fire. We'd assumed the vampires wouldn't be prepared to venture this far—and wouldn't see any reason to. "How do they even know we're here? We left in the middle of the day."

"They might not," Aaron said. He was standing at the end of the dining table, looking at a map he'd spread out there. "They might just want to do whatever damage they can to the property—as a show of force, to lower our general morale. It doesn't sound as if there are a lot of them on their way here."

Marco folded his arms where he was leaning against the table's edge. "Or one of those last few rogues who've thrown in with the bloodsuckers decided to play spy. They might have heard something from outside the walls of the canine estate, the kin there talking about our trip, or simply guessed from the direction the jet headed in."

I gritted my teeth at the thought of those traitors. What had the vampires offered them to make them think they were better off siding with creatures who wanted to exterminate the rest of us? Or did they think the vamps would be satisfied once they'd taken out me and my alphas and leave the rest of us alone? Hadn't they *seen* what those monsters were doing?

Of course, from what Timothy had reported... maybe they weren't thinking very much at all. Sixteen years was a long time to be carrying that much rage. I'd bet some of the losers from the battle at Marco's estate had faded back into the wilderness to live their lives apart from us in peace. The ones who'd run to the vampires—they were too far gone to reason with.

"So what's the plan?" I said.

Aaron tapped the map. I came over to stand beside

him. "There's only one road that can support a truck that comes into the lands around the estate," he said. "Here, between two of the lower hills. So we know where they'll be coming from."

Looking at the lines on the paper, it all seemed very clear. "I go out there and blast them to bits, then."

Marco's lips curled up. "Sounds simple enough."

West, on the other hand, frowned. "You're tired, Ren. How late were you up in that records room?" I pressed my mouth flat against an honest answer, and he glowered at me. "That's what I thought. I don't like the idea of you going out there alone. What if there are more of them than we expect? If they shoot you down, you might be too far from the estate to make it back."

"We have a few vehicles in the garage," Nate started.

I could read the answer to that suggestion in Aaron's eyes. "None of them is solid enough to withstand automatic gunfire, though, right?" I said. "You guys are a lot more vulnerable out there than I am. And they'll be just as happy to kill you." My hands clenched. "Look, I'll just fly up and keep watch. If I see them stopping and getting ready to come out with the guns, I'll fry them before they have the chance. Otherwise I'll wait them out here. Okay? We can't do *nothing*."

West didn't look happy, but he didn't argue either. Aaron nodded. "That sounds like the best we can make of the situation."

"Then I'd better get out there before it's too late to stop them anyway."

We loped together through the halls to the main entrance. I glanced toward the guest wing, but I didn't want to wake up Kylie for this. I had the feeling there'd be plenty more fighting where she could pitch in.

On the front steps, I undressed and shifted as smoothly as if I'd been doing this my entire life. My body expanded up into the air. With a heave of my taloned hind feet, I was swooping up toward the sky.

I kept my word. As the alphas and a few of the guards West had brought along gathered in the courtyard, I hovered above the estate with vast, steady flaps of my dragon wings. Fire itched to unfurl up my throat. I couldn't help remembering that past dragon shifter's comment about the fae trying to steal those flames from her mother.

I didn't have time to puzzle over that idea further. Movement caught my eye in the distance between the rolling hills.

The vampires had left their headlights off, having perfectly good night vision and no interest in giving us any warning. But the moon was bright enough for my shifter vision to pick out the shape of the vehicle cruising toward us down the road.

It must also have been bright enough for the vampires to see me, waiting against the starry sky. The truck had only crossed about a quarter of the distance between the hills and the estate buildings when it started to slow.

I braced myself, my muscles bunching. With a few broad flaps of my wings, I soared closer. The second the vamps stopped or showed any sign of disembarking, I had to dive. I had to burn them up before they could turn their guns on me.

The truck didn't stop, though. At my movement, it

swerved around in a U-turn. As soon as the vehicle was pointing away from me, they hit the gas. The truck shot down the road the way it'd come.

I hurtled after it, tucking my wings tight as the wind warbled over my scales. The itch in my throat deepened into a furious burn. In the back of my mind the echo of gunshots rose up, the jabs of the bullets' impact, Nate's body as he'd crumpled the other night.

The vampires were stretching the distance between us. Almost at the pass between the hills already. No, I couldn't let them escape. I smacked my wings through the air, fangs scraping together in frustration.

A tickle of sensation broke through my rage. A tug. I tried to shake it off, but it wrapped all through my awareness. Abruptly, the meaning of it hit me.

My mates were calling me home.

My muscles twitched, rejecting the idea of retreat. I could keep going, fly harder, farther. I could feel it.

But that wasn't the point, was it? I'd promised them. And the last time I'd gotten carried away with vengeance, I'd burned most of a forest down. As soon as the truck veered out of sight into the pass, the vamps could stop and get ready for me with their guns.

That might even be what they wanted—for me to keep chasing them.

An ache formed in my chest. I didn't want to let them just leave. I wanted them all burned into cinders. But I forced myself to bank on the wind and wheel around.

The smell of clover filled my nostrils again as I glided over the property I'd inherited with my role and landed in the estate's grassy yard. I let myself shift back when my feet touched the ground. The grass pressed soft and cool against my tender human skin. Then an arm slid around my shoulders, pulling me into a tight, pine-tinged embrace.

West. The last of my anger fled as I buried my face in his shoulder. He'd never been the one to come to me after a shift before. But everything was different now.

Everything was different.

He helped me up, keeping his arm around me. I didn't need his support to stand, but it felt kind of nice having him there anyway. And I liked being able to see up close the faint embarrassed flush that had crept up his neck.

My other mates had gathered around us. "The vamps left," I said. "They saw me and they took off. For now."

The last words fell from my lips with an ominous weight. We all knew they'd be back tomorrow, with larger numbers or a more thorough plan.

"Then we get ready for them," Nate said, but I heard the thread of worry in his voice. It wasn't just this estate but so many other kin all across the country we needed to protect.

It was too much for one dragon alone. I could admit that. Maybe it was too much for even me and my alphas and all the kin who stood with us.

If we could summon powers beyond our own kind, I had to find that out.

I took a deep breath and raised my chin. "As soon as it's light, I want to talk to the fae."

Ren

"I DON'T KNOW about this, Sparks," West said as we pushed through the brush in the dense forest. Twigs crackled under our feet. My alphas and I were making our way through the woods on the other side of one of my hills, not far beyond the property that belonged to the dragon shifter estate, toward a pocket of fae land. The sky had clouded, but a few streaks of sunlight pierced through, bringing the summer heat with them even this early in the morning.

"For any reason other than the hundred or so complaints you've already made?" I asked the wolf shifter.

West narrowed his eyes at me. Then his expression gentled as he wiped away a cool drop of dew that had dripped onto my cheek. "You haven't had many dealings with the fae yet. I've never seen a sign they have the slightest friendly feeling toward us. Even the history fanatic back there hasn't heard of any warm relations between our communities." He jabbed his thumb toward Aaron.

That sounded pretty similar to his earlier objections. "Okay, but I *know* they worked with the dragon shifters before. You all saw the carvings on that pedestal in the mountain. I listened to a dragon shifter from almost two hundred years ago talk about how great the fae are."

"Two hundred years is a pretty long time," Marco pointed out.

"I know," I said. "And obviously relations have gone pretty—incredibly—sour. But..." I touched West's arm with what I hoped was a reassuring caress. "We need allies. The vampires are almost overwhelming us. The fae used to be willing to stand by our side. I'm not saying we let them off the hook for the things they've done wrong. I just have to find out if there's anything I can do to mend that falling out—at least enough that they'll help us push back the bloodsuckers."

"You always want to see the good in people, don't you?" he said with a baleful look.

I raised my eyebrows at him. "A quality I think *you* should be particularly thankful for."

Nate gave a cough that might have been covering a laugh. West glanced back at the bear shifter with a growl, but it was more playful than menacing. He elbowed me. "Point taken. And I do think the fae probably hate the vampires at least as much as they hate us. Possibly more. If it's more, we might be able to work with that. I just don't want them anywhere near my kin."

"I'll keep that in mind."

"You really are an overachiever, Princess of Flames," Marco said teasingly. "A few weeks ago we grab you and tell you you've got to unite the kin-groups—surprise! And you've already moved on from that to uniting entire paranormal communities."

I smiled. "Well, I don't think I'm exactly *finished* uniting the kin-groups yet. And I don't know if I'm going to manage to unite anything at all with the fae. We'll just have to see."

"West is right about one thing," Aaron said. "You can play to the idea of their own self-interest. The vampires could easily decide they want to exterminate the fae when they're done with us."

"Just that one thing?" West grumbled, cocking his head.

Aaron chuckled. "We'll see about the rest. I doubt Ren's ancestors recorded events that never happened. But I agree that the fae haven't shown much indication of friendliness in my lifetime."

Well, that seemed to be par for the course for me these days. Taking on the Impossible: The Serenity Drake story. Who would I want to play me in the movie version?

Nate paused, touching a mark on one of the tree trunks. "We're coming into the local fae leader's domain now. Maybe we should keep the negative comments quiet from here on?"

"Good plan," I said, with particular emphasis at West.

He held up his hands. "I'm not going to ruin your

peacekeeping mission, Sparks! But I also don't promise I won't say 'I told you so' if this goes sideways."

I rolled my eyes at him. "As long as you say it while you're making better use of those hands, I promise I won't mind."

His gaze heated up in an instant. "I'll take that deal."

There, now I had him grinning. Maybe that thought would keep him in a better mood until we were finished with this mission.

The fae weren't expecting us like they had been when I'd met with their monarch not that long ago. I stopped a few steps down the rough path by the edge of their territory and propped myself against a tree to wait. The last thing I needed was to start this impromptu parlay off on the wrong foot by barging deep into their lands. I could show proper respect. I just wanted them to notice I was here.

It only took a few minutes. A slender, elongated figure slipped from between the trees. Her entire form shimmered with a glow that made it difficult to tell if she was even wearing clothing—or if she wasn't, how human her body was.

"Shifters," she said, with a slight bob of her head. "Dragon and alphas. These are our grounds."

I straightened up. "I know. I'd like to speak with the one who rules over you in this territory."

The fae woman's eyes gleamed with an even deeper sparkle, like a silver coin under sunlit water. "On what matter?"

I remembered Aaron's suggestion. "A major threat that could affect both our peoples."

The woman pursed her lips, but she bobbed her head again. "I will see if he is willing to meet with you. Stay here."

There was a slightly accusatory note to her last words, as if she thought we'd want to go gallivanting around fae territory the second we had the slightest opening. "That's fine," I said, leaning back against the tree.

"Oh, yeah," West said under his breath after she'd vanished into the woods. "I'm bowled over by that warm welcome."

I stuck my tongue out at him and then *really* hoped no fae were still watching us. "I haven't had a chance to make my case yet."

He sighed. "Well, if anyone can convince them, it's you."

That was the greatest vote of confidence I'd ever gotten from him. I'd take it.

"So the fae have leaders based on where they live?" I asked Aaron, figuring the eagle alpha was the one most likely to have in-depth knowledge on this sort of subject. "I guess there aren't different types of faeries like the shifter kin-groups."

He nodded. "The fae have a unique equilibrium with nature. When one is born, they come into being alongside a plant or natural spring or something of that sort. They sort of sprout up in colonies, with all their connected trees and so on nearby."

A chilling thought struck me. "What happens if they're forced to leave the place where their connected thing is? Like if humans move in?"

"I'm not sure," Aaron said. "Speculation is that they would wither away after a certain amount of time if they were forced away. We have a few reports of fae dying if their connected object is outright destroyed. The tie is very strong."

That meant human encroachment affected the fae even more than it did us. Shifters could get up and move, as long as there was empty land to move to. The fae didn't have that luxury.

A glossy whisper carried through the breeze, raising the hairs on the back of my neck. I pushed myself completely upright. A second later, a glinting fae man appeared in the middle of our glade.

He wasn't as impressive as the fae monarch I'd encountered near Aaron's estate, but I guess that was to be expected. He was just the local leadership. The fae man still shone brighter than the lesser fae who'd directed him to us. He held himself with chin high and shoulders squared. Like all the fae, his body was tall and slim, but he was taller than most, that knobby chin of his nearly level with Nate's forehead. I'd have bet the bear shifter had a hundred pounds more muscle on him, though.

"My name is Cerimon," the fae man said. "I tend to this part of the woods. What is your business here, dragon shifter and alphas?"

He didn't bother with any sign of respect, but the fae monarch hadn't bowed even slightly to us either. It didn't really matter to me. I'd rather just get down to business.

"I don't know how much you're aware of what's going on outside this part of the forest," I said. "But we shifters have come under attack by the vampires.

They've already slaughtered everyone they could reach in several villages. They nearly killed one of my mates. They're using guns of the worst kind, and they seem determined to keep at us until they've destroyed all of us."

Cerimon made a tiny dip of his head. I couldn't tell whether it was acknowledgment that he'd heard of this happening or that he was hearing me now. "And how does this matter concern us?"

I suppressed the urge to grimace at him. "I've learned that the dragon shifters and the fae were once allied." I touched my throat. "I hold the power that my kind and yours created together. I know in the last century relations have been... strained between us, but I was hoping there might be room to at least talk about working together to tackle our enemy."

"*Your* enemy, it sounds like," the fae leader said.

"Likely to become the fae's too, if you stand by doing nothing," Aaron said evenly.

"Do you really think you could defend yourselves if the bloodsuckers took a mind to rid the country of fae too?" Marco asked.

I waved at my mates to stand down. Cerimon was frowning.

"You can say that," he said. "But we've had more troubles with your kind than with the vampires in recent years." His gaze slid to Nate. "What of the group of your kin that set up new homes at the edge of our territory in New Mexico and cut down one of our trees for firewood?"

A shiver ran down my back. Nate spread his hands.

"The fae in that area hadn't appeared to my kin at all. They didn't realize the tree was special."

"It was marked," Cerimon snapped. "A life was lost."

"And we did everything we could to make reparations."

How did you make up for a life cut short? My stomach was starting to churn. The fae leader's gaze shot to Marco. "And your feline kin. I can't even count the mentions I've heard of your kind snapping branches and trampling bushes while they roam around, without concern for whose land they're venturing onto."

"Believe me," Marco said dryly. "I know just how frustrating my kin can be. I'd keep them on a shorter leash, but cats don't take well to leashes in the first place. I do what I can. And we've offered compensation as needed too. I promise you it was only carelessness, not malice. There was no intention to harm you."

"And you." Cerimon's attention moved to West. "Your people took over an entire stretch of forest that had been ours not far from your estate, and attacked us when the fae there tried to take it back."

West's lips drew back to bare his teeth. Uh oh. "The fae there tried to 'take it back' by blasting every shifter they saw with their magic," he said in what was close to a snarl. "And it was land that the last we'd heard you'd abandoned. If the fae had come to speak with me about it peacefully, I'd have seen the new village moved. Instead you killed eight of my kin."

"And how many of ours do you think we've lost to your 'mistakes' and your 'carelessness'?" the fae leader retorted. He turned back to me. "I know you are new to your position among the shifters. I will not blame you for what was done before you had any command over your kind. But I have every reason to feel you shifters can no longer be trusted."

"I'm sorry," I said, meaning it. I didn't know exactly what had happened in any of the situations he'd talked about... but I could see how it had looked bad to the fae. My alphas trusted that their kin had good intentions and that the fae must be at fault. How could I blame the fae for assuming the same thing? I was starting to suspect that if we looked at any of those incidents carefully, it'd turn out the truth was somewhere in the middle.

"All I can do is appeal to our history," I went on. "We've clashed, we've fought—but we also appreciate the same things, don't we? Life, roaming around in nature, lands where we can be ourselves away from human beings. From what I've seen, the vampires don't care about any of that. They probably *want* more cities, more people, so they have more victims to feed from."

Cerimon's jaw twitched. His eyes had clouded. No, he didn't like the vampires at all either.

I felt a brief burst of hope. Then the fae leader spun on his heel, giving me his back.

"This is what shifters do," he said over his shoulder as he moved to leave us. "They ask and they take and they take, but when do they ever give to us? If you want a compromise, any sort of collaboration, I can tell you one thing for certain. It's going to require more than talk for us to believe in you."

CHAPTER 17

Ren

"Stubborn bastards," West muttered as we headed down the hall of my estate to the main dining room. It was early for lunch, but we'd eaten breakfast at dawn, so I was more than ready to dig into whatever the cook had prepared. Even if my stomach seemed to be mostly made out of knots at the moment.

"There's a lot of history," I said. I didn't have to ask to know it was the fae he was still grumbling about. "Obviously a lot of the recent history has not been very good. I get why they don't trust us."

"He made it sound as if we've been running amuck, ruining everything for them. Of course he didn't mention all the times *they've* intruded on us or lashed out without any real provocation. That attack on the lands near my estate? They made a couple of huffy comments and then less than a day later came at us pouring down rage for not realizing they changed their minds."

"Hey." I tugged him back as the other alphas went ahead of us into the dining hall. "You know I don't think your kin—*our* kin—deserved what happened to them there, right? I'm not saying the fae have always been right. They sure as hell should have left my mother alone. But of course the stories they pass on to each other always make them sound like the victims. Everything's a mess right now. But maybe if we untangle it, we can find a way to both be stronger for it."

West's mouth twisted. His frustration showed in every inch of his body, from the flare in his eyes to the tension in his limbs. But as I held his gaze, his shoulders came down. He swallowed audibly and leaned close to me, his cheek brushing mine.

"You know I don't mean any of this venting as an attack on you, don't you?" he said, his throaty voice going abruptly gentle. "I don't believe in the fae, but I believe in you."

"I know," I said. "And good. Because that's all I need."

I touched the side of his face, and he turned his head to kiss me. Just briefly, but with enough hunger to leave me wishing we didn't have a whole bunch of company waiting for us to join them for lunch. My mate tasted more delectable than any feast that could be waiting in there.

West made a frustrated sound as if he were thinking the same thing. "I didn't think I could want you more than I already did," he murmured. "But now that I can have you… You have no idea how much I'd love to carry you to my bed and keep you there for at least an entire day."

An eager shiver tingled through me. "That sounds like an excellent plan for after all this is done," I said.

He grinned. "I'm counting on it, then."

The other alphas were already grabbing food from the bowls and platters laid down the length of the long table. A tang in the air told me deviled eggs and beet salad were among the offerings. Kylie was sitting on the other side of the chair that had been reserved for me, next to the rest of the kin who'd joined us. Somehow I wasn't surprised to see Felix had claimed the spot across from her.

"Are you really going to eat all of that?" she was saying with wide eyes as I took my seat. Felix's plate was heaped with enough food to form a mountain.

The fox shifter brandished his fork and licked his lips. "You'd better believe it. Gotta fuel these muscles, you know." He flexed a lean bicep.

Kylie giggled—her flirty giggle, not her dismissive one. She leaned her chin onto her folded hands as she looked at him with lowered eyelids. "Well, I can't argue with the importance of that."

I raised an eyebrow at them as I reached for the eggs. "You two are getting along well."

"Felix made it very clear that he's sorry he ever doubted my awesomeness," Kylie said, smiling. "And it turns out he's come here to do maintenance on the house before, so he knows where *all* the fun stuff is."

"I hope you don't mind me giving your friend a little

tour, dragon shifter," Felix said to me. "I've got to admit I'm getting a little addicted to spending time with her." He winked at Kylie.

"Better than having you at each other's throats," I said. Although I had the feeling maybe there had been a little necking going on, of the happier sort. It was good that Kylie was enjoying herself rather than stressing about missions I didn't think it was wise to bring her along for. Funny how she'd ended up getting that enjoyment from the one guy who'd doubted her when she first arrived.

Kylie's phone chimed. And chimed again. She fished it out of her pocket to check the messages, her brow knitting. After she'd typed in a couple of texts and read through the replies, she glanced over at me and the alphas.

"You know that brother of an acquaintance I have who works for the security equipment company? They had an order come through early this morning for a bunch of armored trucks. All different spots around the country—but including the cities you said the vampires have a major presence in. They're supposed to be delivered tonight. That seems like more than just a coincidence, don't you think?"

My shoulders tensed. "It does. An armored truck could drive through a bonfire, couldn't it?"

"Maybe even break through our gates," Nate said, his face darkening.

"What about your dragon fire?" Kylie said. "I've seen the way you can melt things. You could still take them down, right?"

"Only where I am. If they're coming at us in those from all over..." I set down my fork. A chill had flooded me, so intense I didn't think I could swallow another bite.

I might be able to protect one estate, but the others... We couldn't evacuate everyone. What would we tell the other kin? To just flee and hide wherever they could?

"We'll figure something out," Felix said, looking at Kylie rather than me. He couldn't have faked the worry—not just for us shifters, but also for her—that was shining in his eyes. "We've never let the bloodsuckers get the better of us before."

Kylie gave him a soft smile, reaching across the table to clasp his hand. I watched them, a slow warmth spreading through me, easing back the chill. It was amazing the way these two who'd spent their first encounter making evil eyes at each other were now taking comfort in each other's presence.

That was how things went sometimes, wasn't it? Look at how West and I had been cuddled together just a few minutes ago. He and I had hardly gotten off on the right foot either. And now the thought of him being taken from my side was physically painful. All that gruffness and criticism had softened as he'd seen who I was and who I could be.

So much angst and hurt could be avoided if you just took the chance to get to know someone.

That thought settled with an unexpected strength in my mind. Saving our kin wasn't all on me and the alphas. I hadn't given our other option everything I had. I *had* to try, before we lost everything. We couldn't understand how the fae saw us—and they couldn't understand why we feared them, or why I was willing to consider trusting them again. But maybe if I could let them know us, if I could show them...

I pushed my chair back. Everyone glanced up. "Ren?" Nate said.

I waved off their attention. "I just thought of something I need to do. I'm not leaving the house. I'll be back soon, I think."

I hurried from the dining hall to the far end of the house, to the door of the records room. The light glowed on as I scrambled down the steps. The two main crystal tablets I'd listened to lay on the table where I'd left them: the one that detailed how dragon shifters and fae had worked together, and the one that explained how we'd fallen apart, from our perspective.

A slanted perspective, I knew. Mirabel had sounded so certain that the fae were in the wrong. But she'd gone into her meeting with the monarch already expecting her suspicions to be justified. Maybe even wanting them to be. If I could show today's fae that I understood our history—

I couldn't bring them down here. I knew that much. If the room wouldn't even admit my alphas, non-shifters had to be out of the question. But maybe... Maybe I could bring that proof to the fae.

I could give instead of asking to take.

My arms trembled as I headed back up the steps, the tablets clutched to my chest. For a second I thought the room might block me from leaving with them. But I stepped out into the thinner air of the hall without any restriction.

For all I knew the fae wouldn't be able to make any use of these anyway. They were precious historical records. If I was wrong to take them from the room, if they were lost somehow...

I looked down the hall. In my mind's eye I saw myself as a little girl, scampering through this house. Never thinking anyone would want to hurt me or my family. Never worrying about who might be coming down the road.

That was what I wanted for my children. They deserved to grow up without this fear hanging over them. If this was what it took to end the threats we faced once and for all, then I'd take that risk. For them, and all the other shifter children not yet born.

I carried the tablets down the hall to the dining room. When I reached the doorway, I cleared my throat. My mates and Kylie and the gathered kin stopped their tense conversations to look over at me.

"It wasn't enough to talk to the local fae," I said. "I need to speak with the monarch. Now, before the vampires have another chance to attack. The jet is still here. Can we fly to your estate, Aaron?"

The avian alpha stood up. "We can," he said. "Are you sure? We can lock this house up as tightly as possible, but the vampires who scouted the place out last night will probably be back."

My gut tightened, but I nodded anyway. "If they damage the property, we'll just have to rebuild when we're done with them. If they come back with help, it's probably better if we're not here anyway. There aren't enough of us to really defend the place."

Aaron's gaze settled on the tablets in my arms, but he didn't ask. West got up beside him, motioning to his kin.

"You heard the dragon shifter. Let's move!"

The sun was still high over the trees as the jet came into view of the avian estate. I watched the property expand beneath us, my face nearly pressed to the glass.

The last time we'd parlayed with the fae monarch, it had taken us a little more than an hour to reach the fae monarch's chosen meeting place, on neutral ground between her territory and Aaron's. Aaron had called one of his kin to reach out to her immediately as we'd packed up at the dragon shifter estate, but I didn't even know if she would agree to see me.

The last time we'd met, I'd spilled the truth-seeking flames her people had helped create down over her and forced her to admit a lot more than she'd have wanted to. All things we deserved to know, but I couldn't imagine she was feeling particularly happy with me or my alphas at the moment.

"We have time," Aaron assured me from the seat behind mine. "The sun won't set for hours yet."

"I don't know how long we'll have to wait for her," I said.

As soon as the words fell from my mouth, the wrongness of them stuck me. *We.* That didn't feel right.

A heavy certainty settled over me. I looked down at the tablets, the crystalline memories meant just for me. With etchings of fae and dragon. It had always been the dragon shifters the fae had dealt with when they'd made their alliance with our kind. They'd seen my mother as their greatest threat... but they'd also once seen the women like her as their greatest allies.

The plane touched down with a jolt and a rattling of its wheels. I was out of my seat the moment it jerked to a halt. "A car should already be waiting for us to take us most of the way there," Aaron said as we all hurried down the steps. "We can—"

"Wait." I raised my hand to hold him and the other alphas back. Kylie glanced at me curiously, but I motioned for her to go on with the rest of the kin. My mates gathered around me.

"What's up, princess?" Marco asked.

I dragged in a breath. "I think I need to go alone. Just me and the monarch. And if she brings reinforcements, fine. She has to see that I trust her. She needs to know how much I want this to work."

West bristled, as I'd known he would. "No. Sparks, it's too dangerous. She tried to have you *killed* the last time."

"Not her," I reminded him. "Some other fae, who acted without her knowing. Not discouraging something like that is different from giving an order. And she swore not to let anything like that happen again."

"I trust your judgment, Ren," Nate said. "But I don't like the sounds of this either. We could come along to the meeting place, but hang back from the actual spot, farther down the path."

I shook my head. "That'll look like an empty gesture. Aaron, I need one of your kin to drive me out there, and

I'll make the rest of the trip alone. I'll fly, in my dragon form, from the road—they won't find it easy to lay any traps that way. If this attempt is going to work, I can tell this is how I need to do it."

Even Marco was frowning. West's face had completely clouded. It itched at me, seeing how worried they were. Feeling it in niggling threads through our mate bond. But my certainty rang deeper.

"I've come a long way since that first meeting," I added. "I can handle this. You all *know* I can."

West let out a sharp huff. "You have. And we do. Just..." He met my gaze searchingly, with so much concern and affection in his eyes it made my heart ache. "Be careful of the fae. And come back as quickly as you can."

If even West agreed, there wasn't much the other alphas could say. My hand clenched around the straps of the bag that held the tablets. "I will. I promise. Now where's that car?"

CHAPTER 18

Aaron

I RESTED my hands on the sun-warmed railing of the balcony and looked down over the courtyard. It was as crowded with my kin as it had been when I'd arrived with Serenity at my side just a couple of weeks ago. But now the energy around the estate was fraught, not celebratory.

Everyone knew the vampires would be back for another battle tonight. More firewood had been heaped on top of the ashes of last night's protective ring. My guards were stalking warily along the walls and wheeling overhead, keeping watch even well before the sun set.

We hadn't told anyone about the armored trucks yet. I didn't want to start a panic until I found out the results of Serenity's last-ditch plan.

Footsteps tapped against the floor behind me. My sister came up to the railing, leaning her elbows on it as she considered the crowd.

"We held our own the last two nights. They haven't won yet."

"No," I said. "But it's been a near thing. If they manage to gain one more advantage..."

Alice's mouth flattened. "Everyone who's able bodied is ready to defend the walls. The scouts along all the roads will alert us as soon as the bloodsuckers show their faces. We've got extra tanks of gasoline; everyone's carrying a lighter..." She paused. "But yeah. I don't know how long we can keep doing this. Especially if the vamps up the ante."

"Well, all we can hope for then is that we manage to up the ante right back at them."

"Yeah." She glanced in the direction Serenity had gone. "Do you really think the fae might agree to help us?"

A question I'd asked myself so many times in the last day. "I think Serenity will do everything she can to convince them. Maybe it'll be easier for her to see a way to mend the damage that's been done between us... She has information none of us had before, other than the past dragon shifters—and she's looking at the problem with fresh eyes, without decades of prejudices already built up."

"There are prejudices and then there's just sound judgment," Alice said. "I guess the more important question is, do you really think we can *trust* the fae if they do offer to lend a hand?"

That was a subject I'd been puzzling over too. I rubbed my mouth. "I don't know. Serenity has proven herself to be a good judge of character so far."

"But she's still learning."

"Yes. She is."

I didn't need to say more. I knew my sister could decipher the tangle of my emotions. Serenity was on her way out there right now to face the fae monarch, the strongest of those flighty but powerful beings, on her own. Our dragon shifter was so powerful, and becoming more so every day, but if the monarch found a way to break the treaty she'd sworn to... I didn't know if I'd ever see my mate again.

"Should we prepare for *them*?" Alice said cautiously. "The fae, I mean."

"How so?"

"Come here."

I followed her down through the house and into the dim garage out back. A truck had come in with several tanks of gasoline. A thick chemical odor rose off them. Alice tipped her head to it, folding her arms over her chest.

"We have more than enough," she said. "We could send these out with a few of our people if we thought they might be more useful... elsewhere."

I studied her expression. "Elsewhere like where?"

"The fae rely on their home ground to survive, right? On their chosen plants or whatever. We could have a team ready near the monarch's territory in case the situation looks like it's about to turn sour. Ready to burn that whole forest down if that's what it takes to give us some leverage."

That's what I'd suspected she was getting at. My chest tightened. Was that what we were going to be reduced to? Preparing to destroy people we were hoping would become our allies, before we'd even tried to work together?

Would it be stupid of me to say no and leave my own people that much more vulnerable?

"When did you become such a pessimist?" I asked, delaying the need to answer the real question.

Alice gave me a crooked smile. "When I realized there's no way in hell we're fending off an army of vampires and a contingent of fae at the same time."

Clearly. I eyed the truck, focusing on the rhythm of my breath. Trying to find a solid path through all the uncertainty around me. I was the one who'd always advocated for listening to reason over our animal instincts, wasn't I? And this desire to defend against a threat that hadn't even arisen yet—that was all animal fear. I felt it with a sharp prickle down my spine.

That was my answer then.

"No," I said, my heart thumping a little harder as I said the word. "We can't enter a new alliance already on the verge of burning their homes to the ground."

"Aaron," my sister said, but I cut her off with a shake of my head.

"Serenity watched her own mother die at the fae's hands," I said. "She's still willing to give them a chance despite that. If she can be that generous, so can we."

Ren

The clearing where I'd met the fae monarch before looked so much smaller from high above. The little pink flowers nearly blended into the green of the grass.

There was no sign of the monarch or any other fae yet. My nostrils didn't pick up any scent that worried me, only the green smells of the wilderness with a faint floral sweetness.

I swept over the trees, the leaves rustling in my wake, and landed in the middle of the field. With a shake, my dragon's body constricted back into my human form. I'd dropped the leather bag I'd brought with me on the ground beside me. I pulled the dress I'd packed over my head and left the crystal tablets inside the bag. If I had to shift again to make a quick exit, I wanted to be able to grab my cargo quickly with my dragon talons.

It was only a minute or two before the towering but spindly fae woman with her crown of living vine strode from the woods at the other end of the field. No delegation accompanied her this time.

I drew in a breath, testing the breeze. A cloying smell had trickled into the air, more than I could attribute to just her. I suspected she'd brought company but left them behind in the forest when she'd seen I was alone.

Well, fair enough. I couldn't blame her for being cautious. The fact that she was coming out here to meet me without any guards at her side, when I could transform into a dragon in a matter of seconds, was a gesture of trust in itself.

She stopped a few paces from me, shoulders back and head high. I'd almost forgotten those eyes, large and stark like black diamonds against her pale skin. The silver blond waves of her hair seemed to clothe her almost as much as her thin but elegant dress.

I supposed I looked a lot less elegant than I had before, with my hair wind-rumpled and this dress I'd picked for ease of changing rather than for looks. But I wasn't here to try to impress her this time. I just wanted her to listen.

"Thank you for coming," I said. "I know you didn't have to."

The monarch acknowledged my comment with a slow blink. "I assume you wouldn't make such an urgent request without good reason. Only a fool avoids information they might need."

Okay, so she wasn't any warmer in personality than she'd been last time, but I hadn't expected anything else.

"You know the vampires have been attacking us," I said. "They've said they want to wipe out shifters completely. They've been killing my kin in the cruelest ways, innocent people who've done nothing to them."

Her jaw tightened. "I have heard of this."

I couldn't read her expression. "You're not on their side, are you? I know we've had our conflicts, I know you've been willing to look the other way when your people have acted against us—but you don't agree with outright slaughter like this, do you?"

I couldn't mistake the twist of her lips and the flicker in her eyes now. It was horror. "Absolutely not," she said sharply. "We will protect our own as we need to, but senseless killing is completely abhorrent. The *vampires* are abhorrent. We have been willing to keep our peace with them only as they offer the same to us."

That was a step in the right direction. "And do you really think you can trust them to leave you in peace if you let them exterminate us without saying a peep? Once they've eliminated the shifters, what's to stop them from coming after you next?"

"That is a matter I have given much thought."

But had she drawn any conclusions? She obviously didn't want to make this conversation at all easy for me.

I bent to pick up my bag. "I think both our peoples will be better off if we can set aside our grievances with each other at least long enough to push back this threat. But I'm not coming just to ask you to offer help. I wanted to offer you something first. I want you to be able to see how relations between shifters and fae have looked through our eyes."

I pulled out the crystals. The monarch's eyes widened.

"My dragon shifter ancestors recorded pieces of our history into these tablets," I said. "Some of it relating to the fae. So that we could each learn from what's happened before. That's what I've tried to do. And I don't like being near-enemies with you when I know it could be different. No one has ever seen these before except the dragon shifters. But I think you deserve to."

I handed the more recent record to her. She looked down at the etchings. "What is this one?"

"A dragon shifter's account of the first major falling out between our people," I said. "Can you activate it?"

"I think..." She traced her long fingers over the image and nodded. Her eyes slid shut. A glow streamed up from the crystal, brightening the shimmer of her skin.

Did I light up like that when I was accessing those records, or was that only because of her magic?

She must have been able to absorb the account faster than I did. After just a few minutes, her eyelids stuttered open. A purplish flush had colored her cheeks. She thrust the tablet back into my hands.

"That isn't how it happened at all. Your dragon shifter then refused to even bring the responsible shifters with her so our monarch could talk to them directly. She wouldn't accept any compromise. And this talk about stealing your fire—we have never wanted to *steal* anything from you."

"Hey," I said, raising my hands. "I didn't think everything she said was completely accurate. I just wanted you to know what all the dragon shifters before me have had to go by. That's how that moment seemed to them. It's easier to blame the other person, isn't it?"

The monarch's eyes were still glittering with anger. "I didn't come here to be told—"

"Wait. Just wait. That isn't the only thing I wanted you to see." I fumbled for the second tablet and offered it to her. "This is the one that brought me here. This is the one that made me think we could do so much better."

She frowned, but she accepted the tablet. With a graze of her fingers, the glow flowed up her arms again. I waited, my stomach clenched with anticipation, as the more hopeful piece of our history washed over her.

This time, when the visions were finished, she lowered the tablet more gently, still holding on to it. A shadow of sorrow crossed her face. "It's hard to imagine," she said.

"I know. But that's how it was between us before. The power I hold inside me, your people and mine created together, for our mutual good. Because the fae once thought that what benefited the dragon shifters benefitted them as well. That we'd support each other."

"But much has happened since then."

I swallowed hard. "Yes. I heard some of the complaints one of the local fae leaders made, just from recent years. My kin have hurt your people. I hate that it happened, but I'm not going to deny it. Accidents *will* happen, but I think there must be ways to make sure they happen less. And to make sure we accept responsibility where it's due."

The monarch gazed at me for a long moment. She looked a little startled by my admission. "We have hurt your kind too," she admitted quietly. "We have let resentment grow. I have let cruelties go unpunished. We should have been better than that." She exhaled. "But it isn't so easy to turn back time. The wrongs done have already been done. Trust already broken."

"I know," I said. "And I'm willing to talk through anything we need to talk through. I don't expect that we're going to trust each other immediately. I just want us to hear each other more, to start with. And I'm hoping you'll help us defend ourselves from the vampires so we're still around to do that."

"You want us to throw ourselves into the line of fire on your behalf?"

"No!" I said quickly. "I, er, was actually thinking it might be possible for you to help us without even extending yourselves all that much. What the previous dragon shifters said, about stealing our fire—the way we worked together in the past, combining our strengths... Is there some way you can use *my* fire?"

She hesitated. Then she inclined her head. "Yes. We can connect our magic to your spirit. Channel that power through our own. That is how your flames of truth were made, with the power of that dragon shifter before."

I liked the sound of that. "How long can you hold onto that power? And from how far away?"

"For as long as you sustain it," the monarch said. "And for a short time longer, depending on how much we've gathered. One of us would need to be with you, accepting it. But that one could pass the flames on to the rest of our kind wherever they might be."

My heart skipped a beat. "So I could be in one place, and a bunch of you could be in other places, and we could rain down dragon fire on all those sets of vampires at the same time?"

Her eyes narrowed. "Yes. *If* we agreed to help you. If I thought it worth the risk."

This was exactly what we needed. How could I convince her I meant everything I'd said?

The second the question passed through my mind, a memory swam up: my violet flames streaming down over the fae woman in front of me. Forcing her to admit the truth. My heart skipped again, in a much more nervous way, but I forced myself to speak.

"If you could borrow my regular fire, then you could also use my truth-seeking flames, couldn't you?"

She considered me. "Yes."

"Then use them on me like I did on you, before." The

corner of my mouth curled up in a slight smile. "It's only fair, right?"

For the second time in this meeting, she stared at me as if she couldn't quite believe what she was hearing. Then she collected herself. "You'll need to shift back into your human form for me to question you."

"Of course. Are you ready?"

She moved back a couple steps. I tugged off my dress, my pulse racing now. I was giving her the opportunity to ask me anything, and I'd have to answer honestly. Who knew what vulnerabilities I had that she might exploit, that I wasn't prepared for?

But I was asking a lot from her people. I had to give in return. And this was the best I could offer.

I was dragon shifter of the shifter kin, and I would not be afraid.

I shifted as quickly as I comfortably could. As always, the flames of my twin fires tickled the back of my dragon throat. I reached toward the violet ones and let them flow down my throat.

I didn't blast them at the monarch the way I had when she'd been trying to march away from me last time. Instead I let them drift down toward her gently. She'd already raised her hands as if to catch them. And that's what she did. As the violet haze reached her hands, she seemed to ball it between her palms, collecting it.

After a moment, she nodded. I closed my mouth and shifted back, bracing myself for the interrogation.

The monarch's shimmer flared brighter. She pushed her hands toward me, and the violet flames streamed from her grasp.

They shot up over me from foot to head with a tight, prickling pressure. Okay, this wasn't being burned alive, but it was pretty far from pleasant. Something to keep in mind when I decided who to apply these flames to in the future.

I couldn't move out of them, couldn't convince my body to do anything except stand there, pinned. And to answer her questions as she asked them.

"Why have you come to me today?" she said.

My mouth opened automatically. The words spilled out, beyond my control. That was fine. I didn't fight the process.

"Because I'm afraid the vampires will destroy my people, and I think working with the fae is our best chance of survival. And because I would like to form a new alliance, with more trust and friendship between us, if that's possible."

"What will you do if we join you in fighting the vampires?"

"Offer whatever power I can for you to use where I can't be myself. And any other support you need to help us."

"And after the fighting is over, if we've defeated the vampires?"

"I want to talk about how we can move forward. How to heal the damage we've done to each other in the past. How to adapt to the ways our world has changed *together* instead of clashing with each other so much."

She paused. "Do you want revenge for your mother's death?"

My eyes heated at the thought of Mom's death, but

the answer came immediately. "No."

"Why not?"

"Because you already punished the fae who murdered her. And I understand why you felt threatened by us, enough that you hadn't punished them before. And I know my kin have looked the other way when your kin have been killed by our carelessness. I'd rather find a way to move forward from all that. I think that's what my mother would have wanted too."

I hadn't even realized that last part, but it was true. I might not have known Mom as a dragon shifter for very long, but she'd always taught me to see all sides of a problem, to remember that my perspective wasn't the only one. To find ways to make something good out of any situation.

The monarch dropped her hands. The flames sputtered away into the air. I stumbled forward before catching my balance. A sweat had broken out on my forehead.

"Does that satisfy you?" I asked.

Her expression had gone unreadable again. "I asked everything I wanted to."

"And what you did there, you could do the same with my burning flames, aiming them at the vampires."

"Yes, as I said before." She brushed her hands together. "But I haven't said we will help you yet. Leave. I need time to think it through."

My heart sank. "If you're going to help, it'll need to be soon. They're coming at us again tonight."

She fixed me with a hard look. "I need time," she repeated. Then she turned and stalked away.

Ren

I COULD TELL the two figures in the avian estate's hall were arguing before I could even hear them. Both of the middle-aged men stood with chests puffed and faces darkened.

Shit. With the threat of the vampires looming, the last thing we needed was to be fighting among ourselves. I hurried over.

"I told you, there isn't enough space," the guy in the guest bedroom doorway insisted.

"There are only four of you in there," the other man said in a growl of a voice. "Your alpha said each room could take ten."

"Why don't you find one with your own kin?"

"There *aren't* any other badger shifters here. My wife and I are the only ones."

The two shifters jerked back from each other when

they saw me coming up on them. The guy who already held the room—a hawk shifter, I gathered from his scent —looked about ready to swallow his tongue. Too bad I couldn't make him actually do that.

"What seems to be the problem here?" I asked, setting my hands on my hips. "I think the instructions about the rooms were pretty clear."

The hawk shifter ducked his head. "My apologies, dragon shifter. I just thought... There are still more rooms with openings... This fellow might be happier with shifters more like him."

The badger shifter groaned. "This is the first room I've found that has space, and I'm tired of asking. I just want somewhere for my wife and I to rest. We traveled all day getting here. And we plan on helping defend *your* estate all night if we have to."

"Okay," I said. "We're all tense because we're all worried about tonight. I get it. But let's try not to take it out on each other, all right?" My gaze settled on the hawk shifter. "If you don't think you can share this room with anyone who's not an avian shifter without squabbling, the four of you can come with me and I'll find you spots in other rooms. It sounds as if this gentleman has been on his feet long enough."

The hawk shifter looked from me to the badger shifter as he weighed his options. His expression turned chagrined. "We'll appreciate your help in fighting off the vampires," he said to the other guy. "Come on, get your rest."

He didn't sound exactly happy about it, but the offer was genuine enough that I stepped back. The badger shifter smiled and motioned to a woman who'd just come into the hallway.

More kin were already gathering around the guest bedroom doors all down the hall. The estate was packed, and the refugees from various shifter communities hadn't stopped trickling in. Everyone had heard about the villages that had been decimated last night. No one wanted to risk being next to face that carnage.

We still hadn't gotten any word from the fae.

Well, if they didn't come through, we'd just have to make the best we could of the situation on our own. And that meant having a conversation I'd been dreading.

I continued out into the common rooms. Aaron was holding court with a few of his advisors and some of the newcomers. I caught his eye and tipped my head toward our private wing of the house. He nodded.

As he finished his conversation, I ducked out into the courtyard. Nate was showing a bunch of the young shifters the best way to quickly take down a vampire at close range. They copied his swipe through the air with their own hands. Marco was giving what looked like a stern talking-to to a couple of bobcat shifters who I was going to guess had been messing with the avian kin.

And West... I reached out through our bond and felt his presence near the wall at the side of the estate. At my gentle tug, I felt a tickle of acknowledgement. He was coming.

Marco had finished his dressing-down and was already strolling over. I gestured to Nate. "I need to talk to all of you."

The bear shifter cuffed one of his young students

lightly on the shoulder. "Keep practicing," he told them, and ambled to join me.

"What's going on?" Kylie asked, getting up from where she, Felix, and some of the other shifters had been preparing a stack of torches with dry chunks of branches and gasoline.

"I think we need to make a small adjustment in our plans," I said. "You might as well come along too." I'd be telling her afterward anyway.

We slipped around the fringes of the crowded public areas to the hall where the alphas' private rooms lay. Aaron was already waiting in the small lounge area there. West came in a moment later.

"What's the matter?" he asked, his eyes immediately seeking out mine.

"Nothing exactly," I said. "But there's something I need to say before it's too late. I think, whether we hear from the fae or not—but especially if we don't—it'd be best if you all went to your own estates."

The last few words made my throat ache coming up. My whole body ached, thinking about it. Seeing the way my mates stared at me in response.

"You want us to *leave* you?" Nate said, as incredulously as if I'd suggested he should fly back to his estate with his arms instead of a jet.

"Well, I'd be leaving too," I said, willing my voice to stay steady. "I think I should be at the canine estate. It's been hit the hardest already, and the vampires from both New York and Chicago will be focused there. So if I can only protect one place, that seems like the one that'll need me the most. And your kin need you with them more than I do tonight. You can rally them, keep them hopeful."

I caught Nate's gaze, and then Marco's. "Most of yours haven't seen you since before this war started."

"Serenity," Aaron said softly. I realized I was trembling. I clenched my hands, drawing my shoulders back.

I'd never been apart from my mates, not by more than an hour or two's drive, since they'd found me. It'd wrenched at me having Aaron gone on a reconnaissance mission for less than a day.

But I'd have my fire whether they were all with me or not. I meant what I'd said. Their kin needed them more. I couldn't hold them back for my own comfort. Then the rogues really would be right about me distracting the alphas from their duty to the rest of their people.

"I'll be fine," I said. "I have to get used to it anyway, don't I? You all will have business on your estates and the other settlements after this is over. It's not like you're supposed to be with me 24-7."

"No," Aaron agreed. "But given the circumstances— how long you were apart from shifter society—ideally we'd have stayed with you until you were a little more settled in."

I laughed roughly. "Not much chance of really getting settled until we've dealt with the vampires, is there?"

"Well, wherever you're going, I'm going too," Kylie announced. "In case there was any doubt about that."

I smiled at her. "I was counting on it."

"Are you sure, Ren?" Marco asked. "I'd imagine my kin think they haven't much use for me at all."

"They think that, but we both know how much you do for them," I said.

The corner of his mouth quirked up, but he still looked sad. "I can't argue with that, princess."

Nate opened and closed his hands as if he didn't know what to do with them. "I don't like it," he said. "Leaving you with just one of us to defend you—no offense meant to you, West. Or to you, Ren. I know you can defend yourself. But if you're injured again..."

"Then West will be there, and all his kin too," I said, and touched the bear shifter's arm. My throat tightened. "I don't want to be apart from you either. Any of you. But my job is to make sure all our kin have what they need, isn't it? And I can't let what I want get in the way of that."

He sighed, bowing his head by mine. "I know."

"All right. Then we should all go, quickly, while we still have time to make it back before nightfall."

I bobbed up on my toes to press a quick but determined kiss to Nate's lips. Marco caught me next, teasing his fingers into my hair as he brought our mouths together. I turned to Aaron, and he kissed me gently before resting his forehead against mine.

"We'll be with you, either way," he said. "Part of us always will be."

The nervous jittering inside me calmed just slightly. "And part of me will be with you."

I wasn't going to let myself think about how this might be the last time I saw any of them.

West had stayed quiet through the whole

conversation. There wasn't much for him to say, I guessed, when he was the one I'd be with. And I knew he had to want to get back to his own kin. But when I came up beside him as we all strode out toward the air strip, he looked almost haunted.

"You haven't even had all of us for a whole two days yet, Sparks," he said.

I managed to smile. "Oh, I don't know. I think I had you a lot longer than that."

He glanced at me with a flash of his eyes. His mouth twitched. "All right. I'll give you that."

"You'd better go round up the rest of your kin who came with us," I told him. "I think my best friend will be particularly disappointed if a certain fox shifter gets left behind."

West chuckled and loped off toward the courtyard. The best friend in question looped her arm around mine. "Always looking out for my best interests."

I nudged Kylie in the side with my elbow. "When you let me."

West's underlings caught up with us as we reached the field where the avian jets and the canine one we'd arrived in were waiting. I'd only made it two steps toward the latter when an eerie sensation rippled over my skin, raising the hairs on my arms.

An instant later, a pale slender form appeared as if out of the sunlight in front of me.

"Forgive the unexpected intrusion, dragon shifter, alphas," the fae man said in a cool voice. "My monarch wanted me to reach you as quickly as possible. I have just one question before I give you her answer: If we help you now, do you swear that you will come to our aid in a similar time of need?"

My heart skipped a beat. "Ren," West said beside me, cautioning.

Sure, the promise was vague—but how could I say no, considering how much I was asking of them? I didn't let myself second-guess my answer.

"Yes," I said. "Of course. I swear it."

The fae man gave me a slight bob of his head. "Then we will assist in your fight against the vampires."

Just like that? It took me a second to catch my breath. "Thank you. Tell your monarch thank you from me too. What do you need from us to make this work?"

"Tell us where you need us to be and where you will be," he said with a thin, shimmering smile. "We can handle the rest."

The sky deepened from pink to purple as the sun sank toward the horizon. The summer heat cooled in the breeze. I moved my weight from one foot to the other, trying to curb my restlessness.

Beside me, West set his hand on my shoulder. We watched the gate to his estate together, at least two hundred of our kin gathered around us and spread out all along the stone wall, as if we'd see the first sign of the vampires there.

Really, West would get a call on that phone in his pocket from one of the scouts down the road before we got our first glimpse. The vamps wouldn't be on us the second the sun set. They had to get out here from wherever they were holed up first. But we knew they'd been gathering forces—and their new armored trucks too.

It wasn't just our kin, and Kylie of course, with us. My gaze slid to one of the softly glowing figures standing near me in the courtyard.

A dozen fae had been waiting for us when we'd landed at the canine estate. Three of them were in my view now. The other nine had taken positions along the wall so there'd be one in range no matter where the vampires struck. The other alphas had reported similar numbers at the other estates. They'd also arrived at the towns I'd told them seemed most in danger.

West tensed, presumably noticing my glance. My stomach knotted. What if I'd made the wrong decision? The fae could decide to turn on us after all, to make sure the bloodsuckers wiped us out, so shifters wouldn't trouble them anymore either.

I'd invited them in. Offered our throats to them, in a way.

It was too late to take back that choice now. I just had to hope my instincts had been right.

My restlessness drew me away from West to the nearest fae. The woman was as tall and slender as all her kind, but I had the sense she was on the younger side, whatever that meant in fae terms. She gave me a faint smile when I joined her.

"Is there anything else I'll need to do?" I asked. "Or do I just have to stay near you and start breathing my fire?"

She nodded. "From what I understand and what my

monarch said, that's all we'll need. I've already tapped into your energy with my magic. When you stir up that fire, I'll be able to channel it—for my own use, and to stream it through me to all the other fae who've come out."

"Even the ones across the country?"

"It isn't so far," she said, as if she were in the habit of taking a jaunt from one ocean to the other in her daily walk. "We are all connected, you know. We can reach each other without much effort at all. Otherwise it would be very lonely, needing to always stay close to our homes."

Oh. So they had some sort of telepathic communication? I guessed that made sense, when she put it that way. No wonder the fae leader near the dragon shifter estate had known about all the offenses the shifters had made in other fae territories.

The fae woman paused. "We fae live a long time, you know," she went on. "Longer than shifters. One of the elders in my domain spoke to me once of sharing fire with a dragon shifter. She said it was the most thrilling experience of her life. I'm saddened by the reason you needed our help—but I'm excited to be a part of it."

My eyebrows shot up. "Really?" I said. "I, ah, got the impression you were all pretty uncertain about having anything to do with shifters."

"Some of us, maybe," she said. "Some didn't have anyone to pass on those memories. There've been so many bad ones in between. But I don't think it makes sense for any of us to be *afraid* of you."

My stomach started to unclench. Afraid of us? Was

that what it came down to? I guessed it did. All of us, afraid of how the other could hurt us, striking out to try to defend ourselves from offenses no one had even committed yet.

We should have been better than that, the monarch had said. We all should have. And maybe we could be, tonight.

"Or for us to be afraid of you," I suggested. Her smile grew a little, as if she understood exactly what I meant.

West had raised his phone to his ear. While I'd been talking to the fae woman, the sun had disappeared completely. The wolf shifter called over to me. "The trucks are on the move. They'll be here soon."

I breathed in and out deep and slow, readying myself for a shift. I'd need to hold it as long as I possibly could if we were going to push the vampires back all across the country. All we needed was for them to arrive and try to breach our walls, and we'd incinerate them inside those damned trucks they must have thought themselves so smart to obtain.

The other shifters stirred in their places around the courtyard. An owl hooted in the distance. Then my ears picked up the distant sounds of engines.

They grew from a hum into a rumble. Everyone along the walls went still, braced for action. The engine's growl rose even higher—and cut off as the trucks must have come to a stop.

I exhaled sharply in the sudden silence. A different sound reached my ears: a low, rolling chuckle that made every nerve in my body jangle in alarm.

"Oh, dragon shifter," a cajoling voice carried over the wall. "Won't you come out and play?"

West looked to me, frowning. My skin had turned clammy. Nausea swelled inside me.

"It's him," I said hoarsely, just loud enough for my mate to hear me. "The rogue who led the attack on my estate—the one who had my family killed."

CHAPTER 20

Ren

"Do you remember me?" the voice went on, lilting over the canine estate's stone wall with an amused tone that set my teeth on edge. "I remember you. Scared little girl scampering after her mother down the halls. Too bad we didn't paint them with your blood too that night."

I remembered. Oh, hell, did I remember. When he chuckled again, the tone of it took me back sixteen years to that panicked dash through the estate, adrenaline sour on my tongue and heart thudding at the base of my throat. To the blood the rogues *had* spilled all over my home. My dads'. My sisters'.

I'd assumed we'd caught the rogue who'd led that assault in one of our past battles with his group. I hadn't seen him clearly back then, didn't even know what kind of shifter he was, so there'd been no way to tell other than that chuckle. But charging into battle wasn't how he worked, was it? He led others to the fray and then stood back to watch the carnage.

To watch and laugh.

So he'd survived. Survived and gone running to the vampires with his last few rogue accomplices? Was he using them to get his revenge or were they using him?

Possibly both.

"Well, then, where are you?" the rogue called again. "Still too scared to stand your ground and face me?"

My jaw clenched. West gripped my arm. I hadn't even heard him coming to my side.

"Ignore him," my mate said in a low voice. "He's trying to get you worked up. To distract you. But he doesn't matter. When we take down the vampires, we'll take down any rogues with them too."

Bertrand jogged across the courtyard to us. "We've got eyes on four rogues. The vampires are staying back, but those traitors have come right out of the forest. Looks like the bloodsuckers have shared their guns."

If they were at the edge of the forest, then they were in my firing range.

As if triggered by my thought, a crackle of gunfire sounded near the gate. The guards along the wall jerked down. One yelped, clapping his hand to his head where a bullet had grazed his temple. A couple of his kin rushed to help.

I gritted my teeth. We couldn't just leave the rogues alone. With that weaponry, they were almost as big a threat as the vampires.

I yanked my arm away from West and strode to the wall. The urge to shift was already prickling through me.

I could at least pick off these few, even if the vampires were still hiding in the shelter of the forest. A little warm-up. Show them how far from scared I was.

"Wow," the lead rogue said, his voice dripping with disdain. "Still no sign of that fearsome dragon. I guess we don't have anything to worry about here after all. She can't even be bothered to protect her kin."

West followed me, catching my wrist again. "Don't," he said.

The rogue kept going. "Just like your mother, apparently. Running away instead of standing and fighting. Not that it did her any good. Did you hear your sisters crying out as we cut them down? And those pathetic alphas—I put the bullet in one of your fathers' heads myself, while he lay groaning."

Rage flared through my body. It pushed the talons from my fingers and the scales to the surface of my skin. A draconic roar rang from my throat as my muscles twisted and expanded. My wings unfurled, ready to cast me up in to the air, so I could incinerate them like so much barbeque. Wrench their lives from this world like they had my family's. Pay them back for every bit of pain they'd caused—

Flames scorched the base of my throat as I tensed to push myself off the ground—and a memory seared through my head. The wild rush of the fire over the trees when I'd lost control after our parlay with the vampire king.

I caught myself, regret twisting around my fury. Containing it, just barely.

No. This was what the rogues wanted. Why else

would he be saying things that horrible? I had to keep a clear head. I had to keep my human reason, like Aaron always said.

It was our animal sides, the sides that wanted to lash out and bite back the second we were hurt, that had gotten us into so much trouble, wasn't it? That had split us apart from our alliance with the fae all those years ago.

I'd chosen differently. I could choose differently again.

A ragged breath released from my already constricting throat. I collapsed back into my human form. West was there waiting. His arms went around me as I stumbled. I accepted his support for just a second as I got my bearings. Then I straightened up.

"We have to deal with them," I said. "But we make a plan first. What do they want? What are *they* planning?"

West's eyes were still worried, but he followed my cue. "They want to lure you out there, so they must think they'll have an advantage when they do. Four guns isn't enough to take you down before you fry them."

I nodded. "And the vampires are going along with whatever the rogues are doing. It might even be a plan *they* came up with. They want to get rid of me before they come at the rest of you." I ran my tongue over the edges of my teeth. "There must be a bunch of the vamps waiting with a good line of sight to where the rogues are. They'd shoot me while I'm occupied with the rogues."

"That would make the most sense, strategically," Bertrand said.

"So we turn the tables on them." I'd learned other things during that skirmish at the gas station. I glanced between West and his lieutenant. "The kin can take on the vampires while they're in the denser forest, right? The vamps won't be able to take long shots, and we have the advantage hand-to-hand. I can pretend I'm going after the rogues, and while they're focused on me, a bunch of your people can come at the vampires from the other side."

"Pretend?" West repeated. "I'm thinking that's going to look an awful lot like actually doing it."

I glowered at him. "I won't get too close. I'll swing around. Their range of fire can't be very wide through the trees. And if a few bullets clip me, well, I've survived that before. We get in there, take out as many as we can in the first minute of confusion, and then withdraw. Maybe that'll be enough to get them to stop lurking and come at us so I can really take them on with our fae friends."

West's jaw tightened at the mention of the fae, but he nodded. "Don't cut it too close," he told me gruffly.

"I know," I said, suddenly choked up.

He turned to Bertrand. "You heard her. Get a bunch of our people, the fastest fighters, ready to dash for the forest the second she goes over the wall."

His lieutenant gave a jerky bob of his head and rushed off. Within moments, he'd rounded up a pack near the gate. I marched the last few steps to the wall and pitched my voice to carry over it.

"Rogues!" I shouted. "And your vampire allies. This is your last chance to back down before I destroy all of you. Leave here and call off your forces around all our communities, and we can discuss a new treaty. Stay, and you're going to burn."

"Big words from a little girl hiding behind a wall, dragon shifter!" the rogue hollered. "I'd like to see you try. In the meantime, should I describe what we did to your fathers after you fled? We pissed on them, you know, and then we—"

I shut my eyes, shutting him out, clamping down hard on the rush of fury that surged through my chest again. "No movement from the vampires," one of the guards reported.

Fine. I hadn't really expected anything else.

"I'm going," I said to West. "I'll be back. I promise."

Then I launched myself off the ground.

The wind whipped over my expanding body. I flung myself high with a vast sweep of my wings.

My sharp eyes caught the cluster of four shifters just a step from the edge of the trees, twenty feet from our wall. A whiff of their scents reached my nostrils.

Jackal. The grizzled man with white streaked hair who was hollering more insults at me even now was a jackal shifter. A scavenger, happy to desecrate the dead for his own gain. How fucking fitting.

I let out a furious shriek and dove. At the edge of my vision, I saw my kin slipping over the wall and darting across the cleared ring into the trees farther down the estate. The rogues raised their guns. *They* didn't need any special angle to get a shot at me. Bullets pinged off my wings and chest, the distance offsetting the damage they might have done. I careened faster, closer—

And whipped myself to the side before I came into full range. The rogues let out a shout of surprise.

Then a different sort of shouting echoed from within

the forest. Shots crackled and bullets thudded into tree trunks. Bodies thumped to the ground. Snarls and the slicing of claws through undead flesh carried from below.

The rogues spun around, and so did I. My heart thumped hard in my chest. While the vampires were otherwise occupied, I could finish what I'd come out here wanting to do.

The jackal shifter looked up at the last second. He bared his teeth in a sneer and yanked up his gun. But I was already pouring flames from my throat.

In an instant, my dragon fire had swallowed up all four of the rogues. Their forms toppled into heaps of cinders. A small part of the clenching around my chest released.

They were gone. The last of them were gone.

But the vampires, our greatest threat, were still here. "Retreat!" one of the canine guards shouted. The kin who'd tackled the vampires amid the trees streamed back toward the walls.

I dove toward them, aiming a burst of flames at the vampires who charged after my kin. Gunfire echoed around me. A bullet tore through my foreleg; another, my shoulder. The truck's engines revved. Forget stealth. They were storming us now.

I aimed one last blast at the ring of firewood, as long as that might hold us, and flung myself toward the courtyard. These weren't the only vampires we needed to deal with. My kin were fighting all over this country.

And I would lend my flames to help them.

I hit the ground still in dragon form, right beside the fae woman. She didn't need any further prompting. I opened my jaws, and she held out her hands. With a heave of my lungs, all the firepower I had in me gushed out to meet her magic.

The heat and the light flowed away from me. I felt it go, in a strangely detached sensation. Felt it rush from me to the fae woman to all the fae around the estate. Felt the sizzle of the fire streaming from their hands to hit the trucks racing at the protective ring, at the vampires pouring out bullets from the edge of the forest.

And onward, from them to the fae to the south and the west. I could almost hear Marco calling commands to his lieutenants, Nate growling as he bashed the head of a bloodsucker who'd made it to his wall, Aaron commanding a legion of eagles, hawks, and falcons.

All my mates, with me even while they weren't. My fire reached them all. Them and the smaller towns and villages where more fae had gathered. More fire washing over the charges of vampires. Bloodsuckers bursting into ashes. Flaring on and on until the sensation of it made me dizzy.

Or maybe that lightheadedness was from the effort to keep producing so much fire. My whole dragon body was tingling. But I had so much more in me to give. So many kin I wanted to protect.

Even as I sensed the paths my flames traveled along, the battle in front of me waged on too. West barked orders and sprang to help the guards by the gate. Kylie shouldered her flame-thrower and shot a blast into the chaos on the other side of the wall. My kin raced by all around me, gathering the injured, joining the defense, fighting with everything we had. All of us, together, bound by blood and history and a friendship with the glimmering figures among us that we were only just rediscovering.

"They're retreating!" someone hollered. Here, or at one of the other estates I was distantly connected to? Footsteps thundered. Fire crackled. My throat burned, but I expelled another long breath. The tingling had faded, leaving only the comfortable weight of my dragon form. Just as much mine as my human one.

I could do this. I could stand and fight all night if I needed to.

But I didn't need to. More shouts rang out, and at least some of them were definitely here. "That's the last of them! The ring is clear."

The fae woman lowered her hands. I let my flames flicker out. She beamed at me, as brightly lit as if the moon had shone a spotlight from her.

"It's done," she said.

I was done. I could shift back now, if I wanted. I stretched my dragon limbs and raised my head toward the sky, letting out a hoarse cry of victory. Only then, carefully and because I wanted to, did I pull back into my human self.

West

IF SOMEONE HAD TOLD me a week ago—no, even a day ago—that I'd be entertaining the leader of the local fae on my estate grounds, I'd have laughed my head off. And then given whoever had said it a good cuff across the head for coming up with ridiculous stories.

But here I was. Walking the gardens to the east of the house in the thin dawn light with one of those gawky glowing figures.

To be honest, the sight of her still made my skin crawl. Too many sour memories. I could ignore that, though. I was man enough to admit when I'd been wrong. And to listen to someone else admit the same.

"We have a long way to go," the fae woman said. "On *both* our sides." She fixed me with a sharp look, as if to remind me that my kin had played a role in the tensions between us. I'd let that slide too, at least this once. "But I am ashamed of the violence that was borne out of what should have been a simple misunderstanding. I hope that we can approach each other with an assumption of good faith... or at least neutral faith, from now on."

"I think we can offer that," I said. And then, because that statement didn't feel like enough. "And I would like us to go forward that way. With patience instead of suspicion. If we can."

All right, so we might both be hedging our bets a little when it came to agreeing to a truce. Old habits died hard. And there was still—

The fae's voice quieted. She stopped and turned toward me. "I must apologize, for the deaths when my people drove you from that grove twelve years ago. Killing is never our goal. I should have been there to temper the panic."

I gaped at her for a second before I found the wherewithal to snap my mouth shut. "Those lives can't be brought back by an apology," I said, but without as much anger as I might have if the apology hadn't sounded so heartfelt.

"They can't," the fae woman acknowledged with a bob of her head. "The best I can give is my promise that my people will not cross that line first in any conflict from here on."

I supposed if my kin started slaughtering fae sometime in the future, I couldn't really complain if they paid us back in kind. But I had no intention of stirring up violence on our end. No, I'd be much happier if we simply left each other alone unless absolutely necessary.

Hopefully my mate didn't have other plans she'd end up dragging me into.

The fae leader motioned to my chest—to the area just below my shoulder where my flesh prickled around the glow of my bandaged scar. "You were injured in that fight," she said. "Our magic left its mark. I could heal the scar, if you wanted. As a gesture of our good will."

I hadn't thought I could be more surprised by her, but it took all I had not to let my jaw go slack again. My hand rose to the scar instinctively. But I didn't need much time to find my answer.

"Thank you," I said, meaning it. "But no. It's a reminder I'd like to keep."

Her eyes hazed with momentary confusion. "A reminder?"

"Of the sacrifice I made that day," I said. And of my feelings, just in case I got too focused on burying them again.

"It is your choice," the fae woman said calmly. "I will take my leave of you. May our paths cross only in peace."

I turned back toward the house. I'd only just come around into the front courtyard when Bertrand came striding over to meet me.

"We've gotten word from the kin we sent to New York," he said. "Just before sunrise this morning, the vampires who survived last night converged on their king. Apparently they were pretty peeved about the catastrophic war he'd gotten them into, and not in any hurry to continue throwing themselves into the flames. The report is that they tore off his head and then tossed his body outside to meet the sun."

I grimaced. "Sounds fitting. So now they don't have a king."

"No, they agreed on a new one in a hurry." Bertrand's eyes glinted with amusement. "The new king has already reached out to the estate to talk about reparations and compromise."

A laugh burst out of me. Damn, when was the last time I'd felt like I could really laugh? I sucked in the dewy morning air, and the last of the tightness around my lungs released.

"Of course he is. Take on the fae and this dragon shifter along with all of our kin? After last night, he'd have to want to see his own people exterminated to make that order."

"Do you want to speak to him?" Bertrand asked.

I shook my head. "Tell the bloodsuckers we're thinking about what kind of 'compromise' we'd find acceptable. Let them stew a little. I've got other things I'd rather focus on right now. Speaking of which, where's our dragon shifter?"

"Still in her rooms, as far as I know, sir."

Ren had stayed up most of the night with me helping with the recovery efforts and making sure the vampires weren't going to return. I'd finally sent her off to bed a few hours ago. The fact that she'd barely protested gave me some indication of how exhausted she'd been.

I should probably get a little rest myself. But that could wait a little longer too. Right now, I wanted my mate.

No one answered when I knocked softly on the door

to Ren's suite. I eased the door open. The corner of my mouth curved up.

My dragon shifter hadn't even made it to her bed. She'd curled up on the sitting room sofa, hugging one of the plump pillows, her face gentle with sleep. Her dark brown hair tumbled over her naked shoulder.

There was a lot to appreciate about the view, but my gaze stayed on her face, my heart squeezing. This woman. This goddamned woman. I'd almost let her go. And then I'd almost pushed her away. What the hell had I been thinking?

I couldn't imagine loving anyone else this much, now or ever.

I knelt down beside the sofa and rested my head against her side. I hadn't meant to wake her, not exactly, but when she murmured and reached to stroke her fingers over my hair, I couldn't say I was upset either.

"Is everything all right?" she asked, her eyes only half open. Fuck, she looked even more irresistible like that.

"You know what?" I said. "It is, and I think it might actually stay that way for more than an hour just this once."

She smiled then, so brilliantly I had to kiss her. She scooted forward into my embrace, raising her head to kiss me back harder.

Tired? Who was tired? I could stay awake another week if I was doing this.

Ren snuggled her head against my shoulder. "I want you," she said, her voice still dreamy. "But I want to see all my mates. Soon."

"That's what I came to tell you," I said. "The other

alphas are heading to the dragon shifter estate now. I'll take you there to meet up with them. What do you say we catch up on a little more sleep on the plane?"

She hummed happily. "Sounds like the perfect plan. As long as you're right there beside me."

I couldn't restrain the smile that stretched across my face. "Forever and always, Sparks."

Ren

Aaron, Nate, and Marco were waiting at the edge of the runway when I got to the jet's open doorway. Suddenly my feet couldn't move fast enough. I scrambled down the steps and dashed into their arms.

All of their arms, all at the same time. With a low chuckle, Nate wrapped me up in an embrace. Aaron was there at the next second, then Marco, and finally West, nuzzling the back of my neck.

Somewhere beyond the boundaries of our group hug, Kylie coughed and said, "I think I'll leave the five of you alone for a while."

I grinned, snuggling deeper into my mates' embrace. Their smells, salty and musky, spicy and piney, mingled together into the headiest perfume. Their warmth enveloped me. The love inside me swelled to meet it, filling every part of my body with its giddy glow.

It wasn't enough just to feel that love. It was time I did something with all that emotion.

"Last night was amazing," Aaron said. "The way your fire reached all the way to us."

"Well, I think it's the fae you can thank for that," I said.

"And who's idea was it again to reach out to the fae?" Marco said, amused.

Nate pressed a kiss to my forehead. "You kept the flames going for so long. The vampires didn't know what hit them when all that fire started flooding over them."

"She held the shift even after she was done with her fire-breathing," West said, the pride in his tone tingling over me. "I think we've got a fully-fledged dragon shifter on our hands now."

"About that..." I wet my lips, feeling abruptly shy.

"Serenity?" Aaron said gently.

I ducked my head. "I was thinking... Our kin have gone too long with only one dragon shifter around. Maybe it's time to see if we can add to that number?"

I'd thought maybe I'd need to be a little less coy before they'd get my meaning. Nope. A tremor of anticipation passed through the bodies around me with a collective intake of breath. "Ren," West said behind me, sounding incredulous and eager all at once.

Marco's lips curled up. "Our Princess of Flames wants to make a princess of her own. I think we can fulfill that request. To the lady's bedroom?"

We walked into the house together, the bond between us making me feel so light my feet hardly seemed to touch the ground. When we reached my bed, I paused at the foot of it. Hunger thrummed through me, but underneath it a quiver of uncertainty passed through me.

"You decide how you want this to go," Aaron said. "We'll follow your lead."

I clambered onto the bed and sat down in the middle of the huge mattress. Then I patted the sheet. My mates moved to join me, settling in a ring around me.

I reached for Aaron first, pulling him into a kiss. His hand drifted over my belly. I leaned back to find Nate's mouth next, and the eagle shifter bent to nibble my shoulder, his hot breath spilling over my skin.

Nate kissed me deeply, easing down the strap of my dress as he did. I turned from him to Marco. The jaguar shifter's tongue teased my lips and slipped between them to tangle with mine.

Someone was easing my dress down to my waist now. Another hand was caressing my breasts. A tremor of pleasure rippled through my nerves. I whimpered against Marco's mouth.

Then there was West. My stubborn wolf. He pressed his lips to mine as if he meant to memorize the shape of them, to chart every curve of my mouth, every hitch of my breath. His fingers trailed over my hip, and the sense of how I wanted this to go swam up through the thickening haze of bliss. From the end to the beginning, back the way I'd come.

For the first several minutes, though, I just floated on that bliss. My mouth moved to meet one of my mates and another's and another's in turn, and then down to the heated skin of necks and chests. Four pairs of hands stripped my dress, my bra, and my panties off me. Somewhere in there I tugged off their clothes too.

Teasing fingers explored every inch of my body. A mouth closed over one nipple. A thumb flicked over the other. I gasped as one of my mates stroked between my legs. My eyelids fluttered shut.

But I knew exactly where West was when I wanted him. I reached out to cup his face. "Please," I said, breathless.

His eyes darkened with lust. He kissed me so thoroughly it left my head spinning. Then he eased between my legs. The head of his cock brushed over my clit, and I whimpered. My hands traced up the lean muscles of his chest to clasp behind his neck. "I love you," I whispered.

He exhaled shakily. "I love you too, Sparks. And I won't let you ever doubt it again."

An ecstatic burn spread through my body as he slid inside me. I clutched him and tilted my hips to welcome his thrusts. West groaned, his head bowing close to mine.

The other alphas had eased back just a little, but they continued their caresses, stroking my breasts, kissing my neck, until I felt as if I were made of nothing but pleasure.

West plunged even deeper into me, and I came with a cry. The sparks of his nickname for me danced behind my eyes. "Fuck," he muttered as I shuddered around him, his voice choked. I felt him spill himself inside me with a hot gush.

He withdrew, sinking beside me to press a trail of

kisses down my arm. "Marco," I said with a gasp. I was too empty. We weren't halfway done here.

The feline alpha bent over me. He claimed my mouth with another searing kiss. His hips rocked with mine, his cock testing my opening. I moaned with need.

"My beautiful princess," he murmured.

I met his gaze with a soft smile. "My gorgeous mate. I love you."

He gave me that familiar crooked grin. "And I love you. Couldn't more."

He filled me with one quick thrust that shocked another moan from my throat. His hand slipped beneath my ass to urge me up to meet him. His cock stroked against the most sensitive spot inside me. Bliss raced through me. I was so close to coming again already.

"Oh, Ren," Marco muttered. "You have no idea how amazing you feel. If it was just us, I'd stretch this out forever, but I won't be selfish."

He sped up his rhythm. Someone pinched one of my nipples. My hips canted up with my whimper, my clit grazing the base of Marco's cock, and just like that I was gone. As the second rush of pleasure swept through me, Marco followed me over the edge with a few quirk jerks of his hips.

Marco sat back, dipping low to kiss my core with a smirk. As he scooted to one side, my hand closed around Nate's. The warmth in my bear shifter's eyes turned smoldering.

He flipped us over, pulling me on top of him. I gasped as my sex slid against his thick erection. When he touched my cheek to meet me for a kiss, other hands glided over my thighs, my back. Nate cupped my breasts, rolling my nipples against his palms until I shivered with pleasure.

"I love you," he said, before I rediscovered my capacity for words. "Standing beside you is the greatest honor of my life."

My throat tightened. I leaned down to kiss him again. "I love you too. And I'm honored to stand by *your* side."

He grasped my hips, and together we guided me down onto his cock. His thickness stretched me with a pressure that made every nerve in my body tingle.

I threw back my head, starting to ride him with all longing I had in me, chasing another release. Nate's hand slid down to stroke my clit. A tongue slicked over one nipple. Teeth teased another. One of my other mates kissed the small of my back. I braced my hands against Nate's broad chest, pumping against him, shivering as I started to shatter.

A long moan broke from my throat. The bear shifter caught me as I sagged over him, a groan slipping from his lips at the same time. He thrust up into me one last time and filled me with his release.

My thighs were wobbly as I eased off of Nate. Aaron was there waiting. He pulled me into his embrace, kissing the back of my neck. "Not tired out yet?" he asked with a slightly playful note in his raspy voice.

I laughed. No, the itch inside me wasn't quite scratched yet. I reached to close my fingers around the hard length of his cock. "Not any more than you are."

"Then what do you say we fly?"

I tugged him around to kiss him on the mouth. We toppled over on the bed together.

Aaron sank into me as if he was meant to be nowhere else—and in that moment, he wasn't. I ground against him with each thrust, my hips bucking faster. My skin was damp with sweat now, my breath lost in panting, but I'd never felt so lit with energy in my life.

Flying. Yes, that was the word for this.

"I love you," I mumbled before I lost my hold on my words again.

Aaron's breath stuttered against my cheek. "I love you too. My first and my last. One and only."

He thrust into me so deeply the final damn burst. I toppled over the edge of that last peak of ecstasy, shaking and gasping. My sex clenched hard around Aaron's cock. With a moan, he came apart too.

Finally, blissfully sated, I let my muscles go slack against the mattress. My four mates cuddled close around me, surrounding me in a wash of affection—and more than a little satisfaction.

"You know," Aaron said lightly, "coming together all at once—it's not guaranteed to work on the first try. Just so you're not disappointed."

A giddy giggle popped out of me. "That's okay," I said, tugging them all a little closer. "We'll just have to keep practicing until we get it right."

CHAPTER 22

Ren

Several months later

"It won't hurt them at all, right?" I said, standing at the edge of the boundary the fae woman had just laid down. Her magic shimmered faintly against the earth between the trees—and then faded from my sight completely. It left the slightest scent in the cool spring breeze, something faintly sweet under the crisp green scents of the forest just waking up from the winter.

The fae shook her head. "The humans won't even feel it. They'll simply find themselves completely uninterested in continuing in this direction." She gave me a small but bright smile. "And you shifters won't be affected at all."

A couple of her companions farther away raised their hands to us to indicate they were finished with their parts. The effort was one step in a plan the alphas and I had come up with after discussions with the fae leaders, to expand the shifter territories without encroaching on the fae. New settlements could be formed in areas of wilderness where we'd no longer need to worry about random hikers or curious tourists happening by.

"Thank you for helping us with this," I said. "I'm really hoping having more room to spread out in will make it easier for us all to get along." There'd still been a few spats between shifters and fae since we'd conquered the vampire threat, but at least they'd been minimal, nothing harmed but egos and feelings.

"I'd like to see us happily sharing more ground again someday," the fae said. "But it's hard to enjoy sharing when you're forced into it. I believe this will benefit both our people. Will we set down the next one near the avian estate next week?"

"That's the plan." I waved to them before heading across the boundary to where the car I'd come in was parked.

Kylie and Felix were waiting there, enjoying a little picnic in the meadow beside the road. The fae's magic *would* affect my best friend, but she didn't have any need to visit the smaller settlements anyway. These days she split her time pretty evenly between the dragon shifter estate and Felix's post in New York.

She jumped up when she saw me coming over. "It's done? That didn't take so long at all."

"Fae magic is powerful stuff," I said.

Felix stood too, gathering the remains of their meal into the basket. He shot me a grin. "The vampire king will be happy to hear about the progress we've been making. More precautions to stop humans from catching wind of us. They're still pretty paranoid about the whole keeping supernaturals secret thing."

The fox shifter was now our ambassador of sorts among the vampire community. Not that he lived right with the bloodsuckers or anything—I could only imagine what he'd say about that suggestion—but they'd given permission for one shifter to live right within New York City so that any disputes between vampires and shifters could be settled quickly.

And also so he could simply keep an eye on things. The new king might not be as eager for carnage as the last one, but I didn't think any of us trusted the vamps farther than we could spit.

"You can tell him all about it at that big party tonight," Kylie said, wrapping her hand around her boyfriend's elbow. Her face lit up almost as bright as her neon hair whenever she looked at Felix these days. I'd been a little worried that moving in together so soon after they'd met might bring out the clashing sides of their personalities again, but I'd never seen her happier.

"You've got to head back right now?" I said as we piled into the car.

"After we drop you off at the estate," Felix said. "Unless there's something else you needed first."

My heart pinched. It would have been nice if Kylie could have stuck around to hear my news right away… but this was definitely one case where my mates, not my bestie, should be the first to know. But I wouldn't have to wait very long.

"No, that's fine," I said.

Kylie gave me a playfully suspicious look. "Is there something going on that you're not telling me?"

I smiled back at her. "You'll just have to wait and see."

She waggled a finger at me. "I'm due back in a couple days, remember. I'll pry all your secrets out of you then."

When we reached my estate, one new car was already parked by the house. Marco was lounging on the front step. He leapt up with his easy grace as we pulled in.

I went to greet him, feeling my own face light up. I'd gotten used to spending days and sometimes even weeks apart from one or more of my mates, but I never felt quite as centered as when they were with me.

"Hello there, princess," Marco drawled. He brushed a strand of hair back from my cheek and leaned in to press his lips to mine. I gave myself over to the heat of the kiss for as long as I felt I could get away with when we had company.

"I've just got to say good-bye to Kylie," I said. "Then I'll be right back with you."

"Take your time," the feline alpha said. "I get to have you for the whole rest of the day."

I headed back to the car and gave Kylie a tight hug. "I expect you back in two days," I said. "Be on time."

She laughed. "I always am. Like I'd want to miss out on whatever adventures you get yourself mixed up in next."

"Keep up the good work with the vampires, Felix," I added to the fox shifter.

He saluted me with a twinkle in his sharp eyes. "I'm glad to serve."

As they drove off, I ambled back to Marco. "How have relations been going between the feline and avian settlements I talked to last week? No further conflicts?"

"They've managed to keep the peace so far. I think your talking-to—and the compromise—did the trick. Until they find something new to squabble about." He shook his head. "We also had another stray rogue turn up, one who was born on that side of the divide, wanting to make amends. The next time you can make it to Florida, I'll have you truth-fry him to make sure he's genuine.

"Happy to," I said. The kin had claimed a couple dozen former rogues since our war with the vampires—and the death of the last of the rogue's leaders. But I'd helped question them all thoroughly first, of course.

Marco slid his arm around my shoulders. "So do I get you all to myself, or is this going to be a bigger party?"

"The other guys should be on their way," I said. "I asked everyone to get here mid-afternoon-ish."

"Well, no reason we can't enjoy this alone time while we have it," he murmured.

I snuggled into his arms as he lowered his mouth to the side of my neck, but he hadn't gotten any farther than that when another engine sounded down the road. "Hmm," he said, raising his head to look. "We can always pick up where we left off later."

I laughed. "I'm sure we will."

West got out of his jeep with his usual gruff expression. It still gave me a little thrill seeing that serious look vanish behind a warm grin when our eyes met. He strode over and tipped my chin up for a kiss without bothering to detach me from Marco's arms.

"Too long," he said. He'd been off dealing with some issues in a few of the canine settlements while I'd been busy with the fae alliance, so we hadn't seen each other in nearly two weeks.

"We're almost done enclosing the new territories," I said. "Then you won't be able to get rid of me."

His grin stretched wider. "Believe me, I'm looking forward to that."

Aaron arrived next, in a sedan that sputtered when he brought it to a stop. A thin stream of smoke trickled from the hood. He made a face as he got out. "I'm not sure which I like less now—jets or cars."

"One of the kin on the estate is a mechanic," I said. "I'll get her to have a look."

Marco brushed his hands together. "Let me at it. I'm not totally hopeless with cars."

The other guys and I exchanged a skeptical look. The feline shifter waved us off. "Just because I like extravagant things doesn't mean I'm afraid to get my hands dirty now and then."

We'd just gotten the hood propped up when Nate's pick-up truck pulled in. "Okay," I said as the bear shifter emerged. "Car maintenance can wait. Come on inside."

Nate fell into step with us on the way to the house, and that beautiful sense of completion wrapped around me. Here I was with all my mates. Everything as it should be. More than they even knew yet.

"What's going on, Ren?" Nate asked. "It sounded like this meeting was a little more urgent than usual."

"Not in a bad way," I assured him. "There's just something I wanted to talk to all of you about, that I figured it'd be best to do in person."

"I'm never going to object to spending time with you, any time I can," Aaron said. He raised my hand to kiss the back of it, his blue eyes gleaming with affection.

I led the way down the hall to my private quarters. In the sitting room, I stopped, motioning them closer. "Give me a hand. All of you."

Marco raised an eyebrow, but my alphas all held out one of their hands. I grasped them lightly with my fingers and guided their palms to my belly.

"Can you feel her?" I said softly. "Because I can." The new life I was carrying inside me touched my senses with a gentle energy like the flickering of a candle flame.

Nate's eyes widened. His hand left my belly to pull me into a fervent kiss. Then Aaron was kissing me, then West and Marco again, all of them closing around me in a ring of love.

"Here's to the next dragon shifter," Aaron murmured.

Motherhood was a whole new expanse of brand-new territory waiting ahead of me, but I was ready for it. Especially with my mates by my side.

I rested my hand over that glimmer of life and smiled. "Here's to her and all of us, and the future we're building for her." A future that could now be lit with harmony and hope.